A PERFECT CHRISTMAS WISH

LORI WILDE

I

"You make a *terrible* Santa. You don't look a thing like him."

Zach Delaney glanced up and found Abby Owens, the ten-year-old daughter of his best friend, Suzannah, standing before him in the back room of Kringle Animal Clinic where he was getting dressed for the clinic's annual photo-with-Santa-for-pets day. A frown marred her freckled face and preteen worry shimmered in her light blue eyes.

"I don't?" he asked, trying not to show his amusement. She looked so serious. "You sure?"

She nodded solemnly. As usual, Abby had an opinion. She was a confident, outspoken young lady, and Zach admired that about her. He was glad she wasn't afraid to express her opinions. Suzannah was doing a great job of raising her alone after Keith had died.

"Not at all. You're a terrible Santa." Abby added a

dramatic sigh and put a palm to her chest. "Terrible, terrible."

Zach glanced down at his costume. He was glad his appearance disappointed her. He didn't want to look like Santa. Heck, what healthy man in his thirties would?

"Thank you." He flashed her a smile. "I'm very glad to hear that."

"You shouldn't thank me." Abby tugged on the hem of his too-short sleeve, trying to pull it down over his wrist bones.

"Why not?" It was all he could do to keep the laughter from his voice. He didn't want Abby to think he was laughing at her. She *was* only ten. As much as she liked to consider herself an adult, she was still a child.

"You *should* worry. What if little kids see you? They'll be heartbroken that you aren't the real Santa. This is terrible."

"We can say I'm an amazingly good-looking Santa helper," he said. "Santa's helpers don't have to be perfect."

Abby released another dramatic sigh. "That won't work. This is awful. You need to look old, and you need a big belly."

"So, what are we going to do?" he asked.

"Hang on." She ran off, hollering, "Mom!"

Ah, reinforcement. Abby had gone to find the cavalry.

The holiday season was one of the many things

Zach liked about his hometown of Kringle, Texas. Sure, Kringle had a bit of a holiday feeling about it year-round, but when December came, the town went into full-fledged Christmas mode. Every street lay decorated, and there was a constant stream of Christmas festivities. Even at the veterinarian clinic. It was impossible not to get caught up in the exuberant fun.

He would have preferred not to get caught up quite in this Christmas festivity. He wasn't a costume kind of guy.

While he waited for Abby to return, Zach considered the Santa costume the vet, Dr. Chloe Anderson, had given him to wear. Suzannah worked for the Chloe as a receptionist, and together, along with Abby, the two women had convinced him to dress as Santa for the annual Pet Pictures event.

He'd reluctantly agreed. Heck, he wouldn't have done it at all if Suzannah hadn't been the one asking, but he'd do just about anything for Suzannah and Abby. Even if it meant dressing up in a well-worn, extra-extra-large red velvet Santa costume.

Suzannah entered the backroom of the vet clinic trailed by her daughter who was gnawing on her bottom lip, twirling a strand of her long light brown hair around her index finger and shaking her head.

A smile curled Suzannah's lips. "I hear you don't have a belly like a bowl full of jelly."

"See, Mom? What did I tell you? *Ter-ri-ble*."

Unlike Abby, Suzannah didn't seem the least bit

bothered by his poorly fitting costume. Instead, she laughed. "Abby's right. You look awful in that outfit."

He couldn't say the same about her Mrs. Claus costume. As usual, it didn't matter what she wore, Suzannah was so beautiful it took his breath away.

She possessed pale blonde hair and deep blue eyes. The kind of eyes that reminded him of the Texas sky in summer. Despite being a young, slim, vibrant woman, she'd done a good job of dressing up as a portly elderly lady. She had a tidy white wig on her head, little gold glasses perched on her nose, and plenty of padding all around.

"You look nice," he said.

"Nice?" She canted her head, that smile still lighting up her entire face, and rested her hands on her hips.

He chuckled. "Let me rephrase. You make a very attractive older woman," he added. "I can see why Santa married you."

She did a little twirl to show off her costume and batted her eyelashes. "I *am* quite the catch, aren't I?"

"Watch out. All the single men at the senior citizen will come a'courtin'," he teased.

She was a catch. He'd known it for decades, long before she married his best friend, Keith Owens. Long before Keith died in a motorcycle accident, leaving behind a heartbroken widow and a little daughter. Suzannah was special.

She seemed happy today. Over the course of the

past three years, she and Abby had healed, but he knew she still missed Keith.

"So, what's the verdict? Can we save this mess?" he asked, sweeping a hand at his getup.

Having Suzannah hovering this close to him was difficult. More and more these days, he had trouble getting it through his thick cowboy skull that they were just friends. She smelled so good. Like holiday cookies and spice cake. What they had felt like a heck of a lot more than just friendship. At least it did for him.

"You need more stuffing," she announced, stepping back and studying him again. "We need to make you look bigger. That'll help. Back in a jiff. Abs, come help me." She and Abby took off.

Zach sighed. Today definitely fit into the "no good deed goes unpunished" category. He'd agreed to help with these pictures thinking it would be no big deal. How much did a guy have to look like Santa to pose with dogs and cats?

Apparently, quite a lot.

He glanced up. Suzannah and Abby were coming down the hall carrying large cushions purloined from the furniture in the clinic's waiting room.

This did not bode well.

"We'll get you looking jolly in no time," Suzannah assured him. She shoved a large cushion at him. "Put that down your pants."

He studied the cushion, then reluctantly accepted it. Then he looked at Abby. "I don't understand why I can't be a fit and thin Santa. Maybe Santa's gone paleo?"

Abby giggled. "No way, Jose. Santa is round and jolly and *loves* cookies."

"But couch cushions?"

"Zach," Abby said his name in an exasperated tone. "You said you'd do this, so that means you have to do it *right*."

He wanted to argue, but she had a point. He also believed in doing things the right way. He'd been a rancher through some tough times, but he'd hung on and thrived by making sure he always did the best he could.

"Okay." He blew out his breath and shoved the cushion down the front of the baggy red pants. He'd pulled the suit on over his jeans and t-shirt, and he had on a belt, but he knew it wasn't big enough to go around the cushion.

"The cushion will fall down," he said.

"We have dog leashes," Abby announced, doing a little jig. "We can strap it to you."

Oh good.

It took some doing, but eventually, the three of them secured the cushion in place. It surprised him that Abby didn't suggest they use duct tape to keep the pillow strapped to him.

"There you go," Suzannah announced, pulling the top of his red outfit down over the cushion and smoothing it in place. They wrapped the costume's large black belt around what now passed for his waist and cinched it tight.

"You should be fine as long as you don't ho-ho-ho too much," Suzannah snickered, and patted his arm.

Dr. Chloe, a petite redheaded woman, appeared in the doorway. She'd dressed as an elf, decked out from head to toe in red and green with lots of bells and a pointy hat.

"Is Santa and Mrs. Claus ready?" she asked.

"As ready as I'll ever be," he admitted, reluctantly following the others to the front of the clinic where the photo shoot was being held.

Chloe Anderson was a terrific vet who did everything she could to ensure that the pet owners of Kringle, Texas, had a memorable holiday by offering pictures taken of their beloved furry friends with Santa and Mrs. Claus. Chloe was one more reason he loved this town. You couldn't beat Kringle for friendliness.

Chloe and her staff had created a nice little Christmas staging area with chairs for Santa and Mrs. Claus. Plastic toy soldiers surrounded the chairs and a fake picture of a fireplace served as a backdrop. Christmas music played from the smartphone that Chloe had hooked up to a speaker box.

"To set the mood," Chloe announced when she'd cued up the music app. "I Saw Mommy Kissing Santa Claus" came pouring out.

At the moment, Chloe buzzed around setting up a table of treats for the after-party. Dog biscuits on one side of the table, peanut butter cookies for the pet parents on the other and paper cups of apple cider.

"Wow," Abby said, her eyes as wide as silver dollars. "I can't wait until I'm a vet and have my own clinic just like Chloe. I love animals and peanut butter cookies so much."

He shot a glance at Suzannah who ruffled Abby's hair and then met his eyes over the top of her daughter's head, worry in her eyes. While she supported her daughter's desire to become a vet, he knew Suzannah didn't know how she'd pay for Abby's college and vet school. While Keith had had a modest life insurance policy, it wasn't nearly enough to cover Abby's education. Suzannah had never actively discouraged her daughter from her dreams, but she did often offer up other career possibilities, but she couldn't dissuade her daughter.

From the time Abby was a small child, she'd vowed to one day be a vet, and she'd never wavered on her goal. Some people just knew from an early age why God had put them here on earth and Abby seemed to be one of them. Zach was one of those people too. He'd known he was born to be a rancher from the time he'd bottle-raised his first baby calf. He and Abby shared a love of animals great and small.

Though Abby didn't have any pets. In the past, she'd had fish and hamsters and turtles. After Keith died, she'd wanted to get a dog or a cat, but Suzannah told her cats and dogs were big commitments and she had to wait until she was old enough for the responsibility.

It surprised Zach to see Ava Miller setting up a tripod and camera. Ava had left town a few years ago, and the last he'd heard, she was living in Europe. She'd gone to high school with Suzannah but Ava got out of Kringle as fast as she could. Not everyone loved his hometown the way Zach did. But just like everyone else in the room, Ava was in a costume. In her case, she'd dressed as a giant candy cane.

"Hi, Ava. I didn't know you were back."

"Just got home last week." Ava bobbed her head and the crook of the candy cane above her jerked up and down.

"Are you home for Christmas?" He smiled at her.

"Maybe for longer than that," she murmured, but her returning smile was tight, as if she didn't really want to be in Kringle.

"How are your folks?"

"Good, good." Her body language said she really, really didn't want to talk about it, and Zach wasn't the kind to pry, so he dropped it.

"You two look adorable," Ava said, nodding at Zach and Suzannah. "You make a perfect couple."

Personally, Zach agreed with her. He helped Suzannah settle into her chair, and then he took his seat beside her. He had to do a little rearranging of the belly cushion when he sat down, but eventually, he was ready for the onslaught of pets and pictures.

Chloe unlocked the front door where a line had

formed outside the clinic and led in the pet parents and their charges. Zach braced himself for puppy kisses and a shower of pet hair. He didn't mind that part. He loved critters. It was just the Santa suit he wasn't a big fan of.

In the costume he felt like a giant dork, but at least Suzannah was along for the dork-fest with him.

Kringle's mayor, Dave Holton, walked in first, pulled by his Great Dane, Charlie.

"Well, I'll be. Santa and Mrs. Claus look great." Dave shook Zach's hand. "What do you think, Charlie?"

Charlie lunged forward, half jumping, half crawling on Zach, and then he flopped down with a loud *hmph*.

Zach struggled to steady the dog, but Charlie was enthusiastic. His long tail slapped against Zach's knees like a metronome.

"What does Charlie weigh?" Zach grunted and clung to the dog's thick collar to keep him still.

"He's about one hundred and twenty pounds." Dave laughed. "A big fella. But he's under the delusion that he's a lapdog."

Zach patted the massive animal. Thank goodness he adored dogs and had three of his own, otherwise being squashed and drooled on could get pretty unsettling. "Yep, he's a big one."

"Seems like Charlie approves of you, Santa." Dave leaned forward and scratched Charlie's head. "In fact, I can't remember the last time

Charlie had such a great time with Santa and Mrs. Claus."

Zach narrowed his eyes at the mayor. The last time Dave looked at him in that way he'd roped Zach into some charity event.

"They do look great, don't they?" Abby bounced on her toes, clapped excitedly and grinned at her mother and Zach. "I helped whip him into shape."

Dave chuckled. "Knowing you, Abby Owens, I imagine you did just that."

Zach didn't point out that just a few minutes ago Abby had called him a terrible Santa. Apparently, the couch cushion had done the trick of turning him into a reputable rendition of Kris Kringle.

"Abby, what would you think of Zach and your mom appearing as Santa and Mrs. Claus in the Christmas parade week after next?" Dave asked.

"Awesome sauce!" Abby clapped her hands.

Hmm. Zach would bet his prize bull that Dave had planned this sneak attack. The mayor had to know asking in front of Abby would guarantee that Zach and Suzannah would ride in the parade dressed as the Clauses.

"Why do you want us in the parade?" Zach asked.

For years, Ava's parents, Ted and Marjorie Miller, had portrayed the iconic couple in the Christmas parade, why not this year? Was something wrong with the Ava's folks? He hoped not.

"Scheduling conflict," Ava piped up from behind the camera. "Kringle Kritter Rescue is having a huge adoption event the day after the parade. They've gotta focus on that."

Her parents ran a local animal rescue, and Zach knew this time of year was busy for them, and he was glad to hear it wasn't a health issue. But still, he didn't want to play Santa in the Christmas parade.

"Things happen, and what we all love about Kringle is the willingness of our townsfolk to jump in when a need arises," Dave said and wriggled his eyebrows.

The grin on the mayor's face did nothing to settle Zach's mood. He was being manipulated yet again, and he really wanted to say no. In fact, he'd do just that, but Abby started hopping up and down like a pogo stick.

"I think Zach and Mom are *perfect* for the parade." Abby enthused.

Suzannah cleared her throat and nodded at the people and pets waiting to have their pictures taken. "Ahem. We've got folks lining up. Let's get this show on the road."

Abby dashed over to a little girl who looked to be about five, waiting at the front of the line with her mother. The girl stared at Zach and Suzannah with wide-open eyes.

"Are you happy to see Santa and Mrs. Claus?" Abby asked.

The little girl bobbed her head. "I've been good all year," she said, her voice low and filled with awe. "I promise."

Abby threw a saucy look over her shoulder at Zach and her mom. "They should be in the Christmas parade, shouldn't they?"

"Yes," the little girl said. "Oh, yes!"

Dang it. Abby knew she had him cornered. She might be a ten-year-old little girl, but he swore, she could sell stilettos to snakes.

He glanced at Suzannah, hoping she'd be the voice of reason and come up with an excuse, any excuse, to get them out of riding in the parade. They'd already agreed to pose with the kids and the pets. Did he really to cruise around town on a float?

But one look at Suzannah's face and he knew she wouldn't be an ally in this fight. Instead, she looked delighted at the prospect.

He started to protest, but two things happened at once.

First, Charlie shifted his weight, making it difficult for Zach to prevent his fake stomach from slipping. Then as he grabbed at the cushion, he felt Charlie's wet tongue drag across his face.

Slurp!

Laughing, Ava snapped the picture at just the wrong moment.

For the love of Pete. He shifted Charlie into a more stable position and turned to look at Suzannah. "Just so you know, Mrs. Claus, you owe me big time for this."

"Good boy." She laughed as the great Dane licked Zach's face again. "Very good boy."

2

"You know I'm always happy to watch Abby," Edith Owens said. "If you ever wanted to go out in the evenings."

"Thanks." Suzannah concentrated on stirring the spaghetti sauce simmering on the stove while her mother-in-law sat perched on a barstool at the kitchen counter.

"I mean it, honey. You need to get out more."

Although Suzannah appreciated her mother-in-law's offer, she knew it came with strings. Edith had been a fairly hands-offs when Keith had been alive mostly because he'd made sure she didn't butt in too much. But in the years since his death, Edith had become more and more intrusive in Suzannah's life.

She'd tried to be patient with her mother-in-law since she knew how hard losing her only child had been for Edith, but her constant hovering stretched

Suzannah's patience. She was afraid if she gave her mother-in-law an inch, she'd take ten miles.

"I don't mean to criticize, dear," Edith said. "I know you have so much on your plate, but..."

But? Suzannah mentally counted to ten and slowly exhaled, forced a smile. "Yes?"

"You really should let people help you more. I know you're proud and that's an admirable quality, but don't let it stand in the way of your happiness."

It was all she could do not to laugh. Yes, okay, she had an independent streak a mile wide, but so did Edith. Her mother-in-law was projecting her flaw on to Suzannah. Understanding that softened her toward her late husband's mother.

"Thank you for pointing that out." She nodded. "I'll work on it."

"That's all anyone can ask of us, right? That we work on ourselves."

"Edith, why don't you join us for dinner?" Suzannah invited, realizing just how lost her mother-in-law was. "We're having spaghetti and meatballs, tossed salad and garlic bread."

"Why so much food?"

"Zach's coming over."

"I see." Edith shook her head, pursed her lips. "That's nice of you to invite me, but I had a late lunch. I'm not starving."

Suzannah didn't need to ask why her mother-in-law had said no. She knew. Zach had been Keith's best friend through high school and beyond. They were constantly together, and now, even three years after Keith's death, Edith had trouble being around Zach. Seeing him reminded her of her loss.

Suzannah felt for Edith; she really did. She missed Keith every day, too, but she had Abby to consider and a life to build for her daughter. Besides, Keith's death had nothing to do with Zach. He hadn't been riding that motorcycle; Keith had.

"You know, Zach's a nice guy," Suzannah said. "He misses Keith, too."

Edith shrugged, and pulled a hurt face, a motion she made when overwhelmed with emotions about her son.

Suzannah gave her a few moments to collect herself. She didn't want to cause Edith to cry, but she also wanted the older woman to stop avoiding of Zach. The rancher had been a wonderful friend to her through the years, and Abby adored him. Suzannah shouldn't have to worry about hurting her mother-in-law's feelings every time she invited Zach over to the house.

Edith gathered up her purse and sweater and headed toward the door. "Tell Abby I'll see her tomorrow."

"She's just upstairs playing a video game. You can pop up and tell her yourself."

"I don't want to bother her."

"You won't."

"My knees aren't what they used to be. Those stairs..."

"Are you all right, Edith?"

"Just arthritis. Nothing new." Her mother-in-law paused at the door. "Don't look so worried. I'm *fine.* Please don't fuss. Enjoy your dinner with Zach." There was a tone to her voice that suggested she really didn't want Suzannah to enjoy her dinner.

Hmm. Suzannah rubbed her forehead between her eyebrows with the pad of her thumb. She didn't want to pry, and it allowed Edith to heal at her own rate, but she wished she'd go a little easier on Zach.

As much as Suzannah loved living in Kringle, she debated whether moving would be a smart idea. She would hate to uproot Abby and upset Edith, but sometimes she felt frozen in time. She still felt married to Keith, and the whole town reinforced that feeling. How was she supposed to move forward when she couldn't overcome the past?

How was she supposed to forget about a man she'd loved from the first moment she'd met him?

The water for the pasta was boiling, and she turned to put the noodles in. It was a combination of a "thank you" and "I'm sorry" dinner. She wanted to thank Zach for posing for the pictures today and apologize for roping him into it.

He'd been a real champ and taken the worse of the wear. The pets and the children had climbed over him like he was a jungle gym. More than once, an overly excited pet dribbled in Zach's lap.

He'd handled it all with his usual humor, smiling and laughing as dogs noisily licked his face and children planted smacking kisses on his cheeks. More than once, he'd looked at her and winked.

Zach Delaney was one heck of a nice guy and lately...well, she'd been having a few unexpected thoughts about her friend. Especially, when he smiled at her in that way that made his dark eyes sparkle, as if they were sharing a great secret.

"Would you like to go to the movies with Abby and me on Saturday night?" Suzannah invited to smooth things over with her mother-in-law. "My treat."

"Oh, that would be quite nice. I've been wanting to see that new Tom Hanks movie."

Suzannah knew that, it's why she'd invited her. Edith had the biggest crush on Tom Hanks.

"It's a date," she said.

"I can wear my new dress that I got from Stitch Fix."

"Do that. Please drive safely going home."

Edith looked a little happier than she had just a few minutes before and she surprised Suzannah by coming back across the room to envelope her in a quick hug before turning and scurrying out the door.

It touched Suzannah's heart. Her mother-in-law could be a pill sometimes, but she was a good person at heart. She just had too much time on her hands, and no one but Suzannah and Abby to shower with her love.

~

"So, what do you want for Christmas?" Suzannah asked her daughter as soon as the three of them settled around the table for dinner. She spread a linen napkin in her lap.

Suzannah was ecology conscious and didn't use paper napkins or towels. It was one of the many things Zach liked about her.

He was sitting next to Suzannah, with Abby directly across from her. No one sat at the head or foot of the table. Zach made a point to never sit in the chair that used to be Keith's. He didn't want anyone to think he was trying to take his best friend's place.

"I noticed you didn't tell Santa and Mrs. Claus what you wanted for Christmas today, so what's on your list? I'm dying to know." Suzannah passed the plate with garlic toast on it across the table to Abby.

Abby loved bread, and she took two slices of the garlic toast. "That's because Zach and you are Santa and Mrs. Claus."

"So, your wish is a secret? If you don't tell us what it is, how can we get you what you want?" her mother asked.

"I'm not sure what I want." After passing the bread plate to Zach, Abby tipped her head and tapped her chin. "Let me think on it."

"You haven't already been thinking about it?" Suzannah sounded surprised.

"Well, the list is kinda long. I was prioritizing."

Zach suppressed a grin and took the salad bowl

Suzannah passed him. He loved how she and Abby ate family style whenever he came over, rather than buffet style like most folks would have. It created a sense of unity in their little group and he'd appreciated the invitations to dinner.

Today had been a long, loud, boisterous day. He had no idea how Suzannah had the energy to cook after all they'd been through. He was just glad to be away from barking dogs and howling cats for a while. The pets hadn't enjoyed having their pictures taken nearly as well as the pet parents expected.

He looked at Abby, who was making a big production of deciding what she wanted for Christmas. Rubbing her chin and rolling her eyes toward the ceiling. Twice she'd peeked at him, then studied her mom, then looked at Zach again.

Why was she stalling? What was she up to? Normally, Abby started dropping not-so-subtle hints around Halloween about what she wanted for Christmas, but this year, she hadn't.

"I'm getting worried," Zach said, cutting a meatball with the side of his fork. "About what you're cooking up in that crafty brain of yours."

Abby frowned and stared at him again.

"What?" he asked, feeling a little self-conscious.

The girl crinkled her nose. "Who are you dating right now, Zach?"

Huh?

The question sounded more like an accusation the way Abby asked it. Zach resisted the impulse to ask her who she'd been talking to. He barely stopped himself from glancing at Suzannah. Abby knew good and well that he rarely dated, and when he did, he didn't talk about it with Suzannah and Abby. Somehow, that just didn't feel right.

"Don't be rude, Abs," her mother said. "If Zach wants to talk about who he's dating, he will. If he doesn't, he won't. Don't put people on the spot like that."

Abby looked only a slightly bit contrite. "Sorry," she muttered, but her tone made it clear she really wasn't.

"That's okay," Zach said, not sure where this conversation was leading. "I'm not really dating anyone right now." He gave Abby a serious look. "How about you? Are you seeing anyone or are you keeping your options open?"

His teasing broke the tension. Both Abby and Suzannah laughed.

"I'm not dating," Abby said. "That's just silly. I'm only ten."

They returned to their dinner, and he thought they had put the subject to rest, but a few minutes later Abby said, "Mom isn't dating anyone either."

"Abby!" Her mother gave her a stern look.

But Abby kept going. "She said you fixed her up with Dad when you were in high school. Do you think you could find someone for her now? I can help. I have several ideas."

Silence fell over the dinner table.

Zach felt like a boulder had dropped on them. Where in the world had that request come from? Since when was Abby interested in finding dates for her mother?

He looked at Suzannah. She seemed as stunned as he felt. He could tell from her expression that dating hadn't crossed her mind.

"I'm not interested in dating," she said, her tone clear that she wanted to drop the topic "Don't fix me up."

"It's been three years. Daddy would want you to find someone else. He wouldn't want you to be alone. And before you know it, I'll be off to college and then vet school. You need to date now so you can find someone by then."

Suzannah sighed and leaned back in her chair. "Why are you bringing this up now?"

Abby shrugged. "I guess because Stephie's mom got remarried last month. She met her husband through one of those dating apps."

Abby's best friend was Stephie Jones, and her mother had remarried last month. But Stephie's parents divorced; her mother wasn't a widow, and even though Abby might not see the difference, Zach knew Suzannah sure did.

"Stephie's mom wanted to date and get remarried. I don't." Suzannah pushed spaghetti around on her plate.

Zach hated how uncomfortable the conversation was making Suzannah. Time for a new topic.

"So, enough stalling," Zach said. "You never told us what you want for Christmas."

"Um, I don't know what I want." Abby squirmed in her chair.

"There must be something," Zach said. "A video game? Some sort of computer gadget? A new bike?"

Abby shook her head. "No. Nothing like that. But…"

"But what?" Suzannah prodded.

"Um…I can't believe how cute all the rescue dogs from Kringle Kritter Rescue were today. I hope they all get homes soon."

Zach knew a ploy when he saw one. He looked at Suzannah and cocked one eyebrow. She had to spot the not-so-subtle hint that her daughter wanted to adopt a dog. But if he was an expert at spotting Abby's manipulation, her mother had superpowers. Zach didn't miss the twinkle in her eyes when she looked at him. She knew good and well what her daughter was up to.

"I'm sure all the animals will find nice homes by Christmas," Suzannah said firmly.

"I hope so." Abby sighed loudly. "I'd hate to think of those great dogs left all alone during the holidays."

Zach was fairly certain Abby was going to be a politician later in life. This entire conversation seemed choreographed to get a dog. He could tell Suzannah was glad the whole "who are you dating" mess was behind them that she'd agree to most anything.

Which she did.

"I don't see why you can't have a dog. You're old enough and responsible enough to care for one now," Suzannah said. "And you've gotten straight As this entire semester."

"Oh, Mom, really?"

"If you're still determined on being a vet, it's time for you to have a dog."

"I am, I am." Abby squealed, jumped out her chair and raced over to hug her mother.

"Thank you, thank you, thank you!"

"You're welcome." Suzannah laughed and shot a smile at Zach over her daughter's head.

Zach chuckled. She'd played Suzannah like a fiddle, but he knew that she knew it. One of the many things he liked about Suzannah was how much she loved her daughter. Being a single parent hadn't been easy for her, but she always put her daughter's needs first. Just like she was doing now. Despite working at a veterinarian clinic, Suzannah had never owned a dog or cat. This was a big step for her and Abby both.

"I swear I'll feed and bathe and walk the dog. You won't have to do *anything*," Abby promised. "If you're right, it will be great practice for me when I become a vet. This dog will be the best Christmas present ever!" Abby hopped from foot to foot. "The very best."

Suzannah shook her head. "No. Not a Christmas present. It's a living creature who is joining our family.

I don't want to consider him or her a gift. We are adopting a pet."

Abby seemed confused. "Huh?"

"Yes, you may adopt a dog, but it isn't your Christmas present. It's a serious decision, much more serious than a game or toy you'll play with a few times and then forget about."

"Your mom wants you to give this serious thought. There's so much more to it than just adopting the first dog who catches your fancy. You need to pick out a dog that will fit well into your family," Zach explained.

Abby nodded. "In that case, I should get the dog. Since it's not a Christmas present, I should get it *before* Christmas. It can become part of the family and celebrate the holiday with us. I can adopt one at Kringle Kritter Rescue."

Zach couldn't help smiling. Abby seemed genuinely thrilled by the prospect of adopting a dog, and he could tell from Suzannah's expression that she was happy that her daughter was happy. It was a miracle actually, that since Suzannah worked at the vet clinic that Dr. Chloe hadn't already twisted her arm about getting a pet. Most of the people who worked at the clinic had taken in many rescued animals. It was most likely because Chloe was respectful of Suzannah's widowhood and hadn't wanted to push her into something that required as much time and attention as adding a pet to the family.

Suzannah had been a stay-at-home mom until Keith died and Chloe had given her a job to help her make ends meet. Keith had left a modest insurance policy and Abby got survivor benefits, but to afford extras, like Abby's braces, Suzannah needed a job with health insurance.

"What kind of dog shall we get?" Abby asked.

"Maybe not a big dog." Suzannah waved Abby back down to finish her dinner. "Since we're first time pet owners, we need a dog we can handle."

Abby perched on the edge of her chair and twirled her spaghetti on her fork. "How about a Border Collie like Zach has?"

"Border Collies have way too much energy. They need a job like herding sheep on a ranch," Zach pointed out. "You've seen Trip and Trap herd my stock. They're intense."

"Yes," Suzannah said. "We need a chill dog."

Abby giggled at that. "So not a puppy?"

Suzannah looked at Zach. "What do you think?"

"Unless you want to do through housebreaking, an older dog might be your best bet," he said.

"I wish Dad were here," Abby said, sadness coming into her eyes. "He'd know exactly the right dog to pick."

At the mention of Abby's father, they all fell silent. During such times like this, he always felt bad for what had happened to Keith. His best friend had been a good guy. He'd deserved better than what life had given him. It wasn't fair that Keith wasn't here with his wife and daughter, making plans to adopt a dog. But life was what it was. No, Keith wasn't here, but Zach was.

"How about we just wait and see which dog catches your eye at the shelter?" Suzannah said. "I have a feeling that the right dog will find us."

"Do you need any help to pick one out?" Zach asked.

In unison, mother and daughter turned toward him. They looked so similar with their light blonde hair and sky-blue eyes. Abby had inherited her mother's good looks.

"Since you've owned dogs, it would be great if you came along to the rescue organization and helped us pick one," Suzannah said. "Thank you."

Abby let out a small squeal and bounced in her seat. "You can take me tomorrow," she announced. "Mom, Zach could take me tomorrow. You've gotta work, but he's free." She turned and looked at him, her blue eyes pleading. "Right?"

For a split second, Zach almost said he wasn't free. He really *was* busy right now on the ranch, but Abby's pleading expression was too much for him.

"Sure," he said. "But shouldn't your mother have a say in your choice?"

Suzannah shook her head. "I want the choice to be Abby's. The dog will be hers, and she needs to find the one she likes."

Knowing he'd lost this battle, he agreed. "Sure. I'll take you. But you and your mom talk through what types of dogs will work. It's difficult to choose one once you're there, and they are all looking at you with those take-me-home eyes."

Boy, did he ever know that. He had three dogs, all rescues adopted from Kringle Kritter Rescue. In each case, he'd gone to the rescue to help and ended up falling in love with a dog and once again adopting.

Going there tomorrow with Abby made him just a tad nervous. He did not want to end up with a fourth dog. He was going to have to steel himself against pleading eyes, both the dogs' and Abby's.

Deep down, he had a sneaking suspicion there was more to Abby's plan than seen on the surface, but for the life of him, he couldn't figure out what it was. But why ask him to take her? Why not wait a few days until Suzannah could come with them?

He'd been a Texas rancher for his entire life, and he knew he should trust his instincts. Those instincts had saved him more than once. Just like he was careful when he was walking on his ranch and heard something rattle, he knew he'd had to tread carefully tomorrow. At the moment, his instincts were on full alert.

Dear, sweet Abby was up to something.

3

"Thank you so much for letting me get a dog," Abby said as she cleared the table after Zach had left. As always, Zach had offered to help, but Suzannah had shooed him home.

"You're welcome," she said vaguely, focusing on loading the dishwasher.

Tonight had unsettled her. Something felt...well... odd between her and Zach. Different. Truth was, she had no idea why she was feeling this way, but she definitely felt off.

But not in a bad way.

She felt a twinge of excitement, something she hadn't felt in a really long time. Excitement, though, made little sense. Sure, she was happy Abby was getting a dog, but happy enough to cause this feeling?

"What kind of dog should I get?" Abby tottered into the kitchen carrying way-too-many dishes.

"Whoa. Hold on there. You're going to drop

something," she said, relieving her daughter of the dishes in most danger of falling.

Once the dishes were safely on the counter, she turned to Abby. "You need to find a dog that you'll be able to care for. Puppies are cute, but they take work."

"I don't mind. I'll walk it and I'll scoop poop and she can sleep in my bed..."

"So you're going to get a female?"

Abby shrugged. "I'm not picky. I'd take a male. I just want a dog."

"We're not home a lot during the day, so it may be difficult for a puppy alone in the house. They need to go out every hour or two."

"Really?"

Although Suzannah had never had a dog of her own, she worked for a vet and had picked up a few things. "Really."

Abby bobbed her head. "Yeah, you're right, and Stephie told me that puppies usually have no problem getting adopted because they're so cute."

"True." Suzannah rinsed one of the serving bowls and placing it in the bottom rack of the dishwasher. "They're cute until they eat your shoes or gnaw the baseboards."

"Why would they gnaw the baseboards?"

"I don't know, but Mr. Teague brought his beagle because he was sick—"

"You mean Baron Von Bismark?"

"Yes, Baron Von Bismark." Mr. Teague wanted

everyone to call the beagle by his full name, but when he wasn't around, Chloe secretly called the dog Busy, because he was always busy getting into trouble.

"So, what happened to Baron Von Bismark?" Abby rested her elbows on the bar and then rested her chin in her upturned palms.

"Dr. Chloe did an X-ray, and she found a chunk of wood in the dog's stomach because Baron Von Bismark chewed up the baseboards in the mudroom where Mr. Teague left him while he was at work."

"Wow."

"Dogs—and puppies even more so—need training and exercise so they don't dig holes and chew up things. They can be pretty destructive if they don't get the attention they need. If you don't give them proper exercise, training and attention then hold on to your hat because they'll eat it."

Abby wasn't the only one laughing. Suzannah felt happy, truly happy, watching her daughter giggle about the dog. "I'm so glad Zach is taking me to get a dog tomorrow. I can't wait."

"Me either."

"It's nice of him."

"He's a nice man." Suzannah smiled.

Abby fell silent a moment, then said, "Mom, why don't you date? You'll never get married again if you don't date."

Suzannah had been rinsing a plate in the sink, but now she stopped and looked at her daughter. For a moment, she considered giving a short, easy answer about being busy, but Abby deserved better than a flippant response.

"It's hard, Abby. I miss your dad a lot," she admitted.

"I miss him too. Do you think he wouldn't have wanted you to get married again? Is that it?"

Suzannah wasn't sure where this sudden curiosity was coming from. "No. I'm sure he would have wanted me to fall in love again."

"You should date then so you can fall in love," Abby said, sounding much wiser than her years. "When Stephie's mom started dating again, she got to go to romantic restaurants. You could do that, too."

Suzannah smiled despite herself. "I'm fine, thanks. I don't need to go to romantic restaurants and meet new men."

"It would be fun."

"I'm sure it would be, but I'm just not ready to date."

Abby rubbed her hands and, looked anxious, so Suzannah changed the subject. "What will be fun is the dog you're getting."

"Mom, please go on a date. Please? Just one and see how it goes? For me?"

"Abby honey, I—"

"Just one. If it goes badly, then you can quit. You don't even have to go out with a stranger. You could date someone you know. Like Zach."

"What?" A strange sensation passed through

Suzannah. Abby was trying to fix her up with Zach?

"Sweetheart, Zach and I are just friends."

"So going out with him should be no big deal, right? It's just to dip your toe back in the dating pool. You'll just be hanging out with your friend."

"We hang out all the time."

"With me around. You never hang out with Zach by yourself. Besides, you deserve a nice night out."

"Abby—"

"*Mom.*" Abby folded her arms over her chest. "You're always telling me that I should at least try something before deciding it's not right for me. Just give dating a try."

Suzannah leaned against the kitchen counter, completely baffled at what to say to her daughter.

"Well?"

"I'll think about it."

"But—"

"That's the best you're going to get. Now give me a hug and scoot off to bed." Suzannah gave Abby a big bear hug. "And dream of sugar plums and puppy dogs dancing in your head."

Abby giggled.

Suzannah kissed her daughter's forehead and playfully swatted her bottom. "Don't forget to brush your teeth."

"*Mom.*" Abby rolled her eyes. "I'm not five. I *always* brush my teeth."

"Just making sure. Go on. In a jiff, I'll come up to

tuck you in." Smiling, Suzannah watched her daughter bounce up the stairs.

For so long, she'd felt like a cloud had covered her. Missing Keith ate at her, and even though it had been three years, she still thought of him every day. They'd had such a great marriage. Losing him had almost killed her. If it hadn't been for her daughter, she could have easily slipped into clinical depression. It was only now that it felt as if she could breathe a little deeper. She'd finally stopped waiting for Keith to walk through the door or listening for the sound of his voice.

Abby missed her father too, but her wise-beyond-her-years daughter also knew that they both needed to move forward. They'd never forget Keith or stop loving him, but they couldn't live in the past. It was just too painful and stunted their growth.

The dog, whatever one Abby picked, would help them move forward into their future. And that thought thrilled Suzannah.

As did having Zach in their lives.

That's when Suzannah realized something monumental. Something that was at the root of this shiny new happiness. Zach was rapidly becoming the person she most relied on for support, comfort and advice.

Secretly, she'd love going out on a date with him.

And that scared her.

Right down to the tips of her toes.

The following morning when Abby climbed into his truck, Zach knew, deep in his bones, that the girl was up to something.

"I don't see why I can't sit up front." Abby got into the backseat, slipped off her bulky winter coat and buckled her seatbelt. "I'm almost old enough."

Zach laughed. They had this argument every time he drove her anywhere. "You're only ten. Sitting up front is not safe for you."

"Aww, c'mon. We're only going to the rescue. We'll barely be on the highway.

"It's also against the law."

"Fine," she huffed. "At least getting a dog will be fun."

"That's the spirit."

Not one to pout for long, Abby brightened. "I'm really excited about getting a dog. Mom is too. You should have seen her last night after you left. She was laughing and smiling and super happy."

"Why the sudden push for a dog?" he asked as he drove out of town and headed to Kringle Kritter Rescue on Caleb Sutton's ranch.

"It's not sudden. I've wanted one for years, but Mom said I wasn't old enough to take responsibility, but now I am."

"Fess up. There's something more going on here than just getting a dog. What are you up to, Abby?"

She was silent for so long that Zach thought she hadn't heard him. "Abs?"

Finally, she blurted, "I want you to fall in love with my mom and marry her. It's my real Christmas wish."

Since they were already on Caleb Sutton's ranch near the rescue and there were no other vehicles in sight, Zach pulled over and stopped the truck.

"What?" Had he heard her correctly?

Abby took a deep breath, and the words flew out of her. "I have a daddy who lives in Heaven, but I'd also like a daddy who lives right here in Kringle with me and Mom."

The air whooshed out of Zach's lungs. He felt like someone had sucker-punched him in the gut. Where had this come from?

"Abby—"

"I've wanted this for a long time, and I've wished on stars and birthday cake candles and pulley bones, and I threw pennies in wishing wells. None of it worked, so I figured I would make a Christmas wish and then ask you to fulfill it."

He sat for several long moments, trying to decide what to say.

Abby sighed loudly. "Sorry. I guess I shouldn't have told you my real wish."

"No, no, I'm glad you did so we can discuss it."

"Stephie said it would make you mad."

"I'm not mad. I'm..." What was he? Worried? Frustrated. Concerned? All the above, but underneath that was something more. Something heavy and lonely. An emotional rock he was afraid to kick over.

"Please don't tell Mom. I don't want to upset her."

"I don't keep secrets from your mother and you shouldn't either. Secrets aren't a good thing. They keep people from communicating openly and honestly."

"Then I did good by telling you?"

"You did good."

"From that frown on your face I didn't know if I did the right thing or not, but I had to tell you. I just had to, Zach. I like you bunches and bunches."

"I like you too, Abby." Except it was more than just like. He couldn't love the girl more if she was his own child. But he feared coming right out and saying that. It would complicate things too much.

And here you are cautioning her against secrets?

Not the same thing. Not at all.

Yeah? Who you trying to kid? Zach turned in his seat so he could watch Abby's face.

She looked so earnest and filled with hope. She beamed at him and pressed her palms together beseechingly.

Zach felt as if a giant hand had wrapped around his heart and squeezed.

Hard.

"Honey, you know I adore you and your mother. I will always be there for you whenever you need anything," he murmured. "No matter what."

"That's not the same. I want you to fall in love with Mom and marry her."

"Abs, you can't force people to fall in love."

"Mom likes you. I know you like her too. Daddy used to tease that he stole her away from you."

"That's not quite right," Zach explained. Maybe he shouldn't be telling this to a ten-year-old, but he wanted to set the record straight. "I saw your mom the first day she transferred to Kringle High School, and I told your dad that I was going to ask her out. Before I could stop him, your dad walked right up and asked her first."

"That's sad," Abby said.

Zach didn't want her getting the wrong idea. "Abby, it's great that your dad asked your mom out first. They were really in love. Plus, it's a good thing he did because that's why you're here. You are so much like him. When you want something, you take the bull by the horns and go after it."

Abby nodded solemnly. "But wasn't your heart broken?"

"I wasn't in love with your mom, not the way your dad was. I thought she was pretty, so I wanted to ask her out. But I was a teenager. I thought lots of girls were pretty. After your dad asked your mom out, I simply went and asked out another girl."

Which was true. He'd dated a lot during high school, and even after high school, he'd dated often. The last few years he'd slowed down, but that was because he was busy with his ranch and making sure

Suzannah and Abby had everything they needed since Keith died.

"Mom's still really pretty," Abby said, hope in her voice.

Abby was right. Suzannah was beautiful, but that wasn't the only reason Zach liked her. He liked her smile, and her sense of humor, and her caring nature. She was a smart, determined lady, and he admired her deeply.

"You think Mom is pretty, don't you think?" Abby prodded.

"Yes, she's pretty, Abby. But your mom and I are just friends."

"But you could be more than friends, right? If you really wanted to."

"Have you spoken to your mom about this?

Abby's smile collapsed like a sandcastle hit by an ocean wave. "I try to talk to her, but she always changes the subject."

"Maybe that means she doesn't want to talk about it."

"But *I* want to talk about it."

"Could you come right out and tell her that?"

Abby tapped her bottom lip with her index finger. "Maybe. I know she likes you. She hangs out with you all the time."

"You both hang out with me," Zach pointed out. "I'm friends with both of you, and friends hang out together."

"That's it?" She looked disappointed and defeated.

"I'm afraid that's all it is. We're *friends* and nothing more."

Abby flopped back against the seat and started fiddling with her seatbelt. "I thought you would help."

"You need to talk to your mom," he said, deciding it was past time for him to end this conversation. He had to make her understand that she couldn't simply wish for something like this.

"I've tried lots of times to talk to Mom about her getting a boyfriend and dating and stuff. She always says she's not ready." Abby looked him dead in the eyes.

"Then maybe you should honor that. I know it's not what you want to hear, but sometimes life doesn't turn out the way we plan."

"I know that. If it did, Dad would be alive." The wistfulness in her voice broke his heart.

"Yeah," he said, because his heart broke too. He'd loved Keith like a brother.

"I know that Mom loved Daddy, and she still does. I still love Daddy too. But he's gone, and he's not be coming back. She needs to find someone else to love so she's not so lonely. She needs a husband, and I think you're the best man for the job."

Her comment was both sad and funny. Although he knew how much they both loved Keith, he wasn't sure "you're the best person for the job" counted for love and marriage. He didn't want to be the best person for the job. He wanted to be special. To be loved fully for who he was. Not a pale stand-in for a dead guy.

"Mom told me she'd consider going on a date with you," Abby said. "You should ask her out. I think she'd say 'yes'."

"What?" A flicker of warm hope flared in his heart. "When did she say that?"

"Last night. After you left."

He started to ask Abby a few questions and then stopped. He shouldn't put Abby in between him and her mother. He wasn't seventeen, and this wasn't high school. "Talk to your mom, and I'll talk to her, too."

She gave him a look that did nothing to reassure him and then settled back in her seat. "Okay, but you talk to her first."

A million responses crowded his brain, but he finally let it go. He felt tangled up in a giant spider's web, and all he wanted was to cut himself free.

Zach put the truck in gear and headed toward Kringle Kritter Rescue. Yep, he'd been right all along. Abby was up to something. Unfortunately, now that he knew what it was, Zach had to address it.

And he couldn't help thinking Abby's wild Christmas wish would forever impact his relationship with his best friend's widow.

4

"Mom! Mom!"

Suzannah looked up from the computer where she was entering data at her desk in the Kringle Animal Clinic to see her daughter bursting through the door.

"She's not exactly what we talked about, but you're going to love her!" Abby exclaimed, her face flushed and smiling.

"Who am I going to love?" Suzannah asked, momentarily confused because she'd been so deeply focused on her work.

"She needed a home more than any of the other dogs." Abby bounced on the balls of her feet.

"Okay, so where is she?" Abby and Zach were to bring the new dog in so Dr. Chloe could check her out. Suzannah pushed back her chair, got up and walked around the counter. "Did you adopt an invisible dog?"

Abby laughed. "No, Zach is bringing her in. She's terrified. She's shivering all over."

"Lots of dogs fear the vet," Suzannah said. "That's normal."

"No, Betty fears *everything.*"

"Betty?"

Abby bobbed her head. "Yep. I don't really like it, but that's her name, and she's too old for me to give her a new one now."

Suzannah bit her lip and craned her neck to peer through the window into the parking lot. Before Abby had left this morning, they had discussed getting a younger dog that was safely past the puppy stage. Obviously, her daughter's heart had led her in a different direction.

"Let me meet her." Suzannah pushed out the door and headed into the small grassy area in front of the clinic. In the middle of the grass, Zach hunkered down talking to a small dog.

"Hey there, old girl," he murmured, petting her. "It will be okay. I promise."

"Hi, Zach." Suzannah walked over to where he crouched beside the animal, blocking her view of the dog.

When she got closer, she saw that Betty was small and brown and of no discernable breed and terrified. When Zach stood, she started shaking even harder.

"You poor thing," he soothed and picked her up. As he held her close to his chest, the dog seemed to relax a little, and the shaking went from earthquake to mere tremor.

"Betty, why are you so scared?" Suzannah started to reach out to pet her, she remembered what Dr. Chloe had taught her about interacting with frightened dogs and she put out the back of her hand for Betty to sniff.

The dog sank deeper into Zach's arms, but after a moment, she delicately leaned forward to sniff Suzannah's hand.

Slowly, Suzannah eased her hand closer until she could scratch under Betty's chin and the little dog seemed to like that.

"Someone found Betty abandoned on the side of the road. They think someone dumped her," Abby explained.

"That's such a shame." Suzannah clicked her tongue, sympathy for the poor creature swelled against her heart. "But if they found her on the side of the road, how do they know her name is Betty?"

Abby looked surprised. "I don't know. I didn't think to ask. Maybe they just named her at the rescue because she's been there so long."

"Did you think she's just lost and not abandoned? Did they wand her for a chip?" Suzannah asked. These days most pet owners had chips implanted in their dogs so they could trace them if they ever went missing.

"She didn't have a chip," Zach said. "They tried to

find an owner but couldn't locate one. She'd been at the shelter for over a year."

"Can I hold her?" Abby looked up at Zach. "I want her to know she'll never have to fear getting dumped ever again."

"Easy does it," he said, gently transferring the dog into Abby's outstretched hands.

Abby wrapped both arms around Betty, drew her against her chest, held on tight and kissed the top of the dog's head.

"I'm so proud of your daughter," Zach said, stepping back to join Suzannah. "She bypassed the cute puppies and instead asked Ava's parents which dog most needed a home. Abby's got a heart the size of Texas."

Betty snuggled in Abby's arm, her brown eyes filled with relief as she licked her cheek. "Betty really, really needs a home."

"Good work, kiddo," Suzannah said, not the least bit surprised by Abby's generosity. She was her father's daughter.

"Wanna hold her, Mom?"

"She looks pretty comfortable right where she is."

"But she needs to get to know other people and..." She wrinkled her nose at Zach. "What was it they said about Betty?"

"That she needed socialization," Zach said.

"Oh, yeah. She needs to be around lots of people and pets so she can socialize. That will give her confidence and help her not to be so scared." Abby peered into Betty's face. "Isn't that right, Betty?"

"All right then." Suzannah held out her arms.

Abby handed the dog to her.

Suzannah held her close and Betty licked the underside of Suzannah's chin, her tremors lessened. She laughed. The dog really was a sweetheart. Betty weighed about ten pounds and had short light brown fur and deep brown eyes. She was a mix of a few breeds and looked more than a little scrawny.

"I think she needs to put on some weight," Suzannah said. "Let's take her inside and get Dr. Chloe to check her out."

When they went inside, they discovered Dr. Chloe at the desk, already expecting them, a purple stethoscope dangling from around her neck. Purple was Chloe's favorite color.

Betty started shivering all over again.

"What have we got here?" Chloe asked, drawing closer. "Aww, sweetheart. It's okay." To Suzannah, she said, "Could you put her on the scale, please?"

Suzannah eased her down onto the scale. Betty looked up at her with forlorn eyes. "I'm right here," she soothed.

"She is a cutie pie. What's her name?" Chloe studied the scale. It registered at nine pounds and six ounces. Chloe shook her head and wrote something down on a chart.

"Her name is Betty," Abby said. "We just got her from Kringle Kritter Rescue. Is she okay?"

"Let's find out." Chloe picked up Betty and carried her into the exam room. Suzannah, Zach and Abby all followed her in.

For the next few minutes, the vet gave Betty a thorough exam. Suzannah helped, praying that Betty would be okay. She could tell her daughter was already attached to the dog, and the last thing Abby needed was another loss.

"Betty is about nine years old," Dr. Chloe said.

"How old is that in dog years?" Abby screwed her mouth up as if trying to calculate the math in her head.

"Sixty-three."

"The same age as Grandma?" Abby's eyes widened.

"Don't tell that to Edith," Suzannah cautioned with a laugh. "I don't know if she would appreciate it."

"Why not? Betty is awesome."

"She's a little underweight," Chloe went on. "But otherwise, Betty looks very healthy. You just need to convince her to eat. I'll outline a schedule for you and place her on a special diet."

"She's okay?" Abby asked.

"She's perfect," Chloe announced, then turned to the computer to complete the paperwork on the dog.

A small smile had been lurking around Abby's mouth, but now it burst free. She gave Betty a big hug. Even though it had only been a few hours, the dog became smitten with Abby, a feeling that was mutual.

"I'd say you should give her lots of love, too, but I can see you've got that covered," Chloe teased.

Abby hugged her dog close. "I will. I'll make sure she gets lots and lots of love."

While Chloe discussed with Abby when and what to feed Betty, Suzannah turned and looked for Zach. She'd been so caught up with her daughter and the dog that she hadn't noticed he'd slipped out. She left the exam room, wanting to thank him for his help.

"Hey," she said, finding him in the lobby. "There you are."

Zach sauntered over. He had such a relaxed way of walking and being around him instantly calmed Suzannah. "So how is Betty?"

She smiled at him and felt her whole face light up. Zach was such a great guy, and it always made her happy to see him. "She's fine. I'm so relieved."

"I'm glad she's good. Betty's a sweet dog, and your daughter is a really sweet kid," he said. "She was adamant about adopting a dog that would be the hardest to place."

"Keith was like that." Suzannah's smile wavered a bit.

Zach's eyes met hers. "So are you."

And so was Zach. He was the most loyal, considerate man she'd known outside of her late husband.

"And you're a terrific friend and a good sport. Thank you for taking her," she said, leaning forward and giving him a hug. "This is something she'll remember forever."

Zach's warm hug made her feel safe and protected, as it always did. But this time, though, she felt something else. Her skin tingled and her pulse quickened and suddenly she had trouble inhaling. The sandalwood scent of his soap with a peppermint flavor underneath. The shape of his muscled arms as they wrapped around her. The tickle of his breath against her skin.

There was an attraction there and she couldn't deny it. Should she go on a date with Zach? The thought was electrifying.

Shaken, she quickly dropped her arms and moved back. "Um, thanks again."

Zach seemed equally thrown. He glanced at her and then looked away. After a few awkward moments, his gaze caught hers and he looked serious. "I need to tell you something."

"Oh?" She pasted on a bright smile past the knot of anxiety scaling her throat.

"It's about Abby."

Suzannah's heart clutched and her smile faded. "What is it?"

"This morning..." He paused. He was a straightforward man, and it wasn't like him to hee-haw. His hesitating worried her.

"What's wrong?"

"I just thought you should know Abby told me this morning that her true Christmas wish is for us to get married."

It took a moment for that to register. Suzannah felt the air whoosh from her lungs. When had one date progressed to getting married? She was going to have a long talk with her daughter.

"What? I told her I would think about going on a date and she suggested I start with someone comfortable and nonthreatening like you. I do not know how that child made the wild leap to us getting married."

"Nonthreatening?" He did not look amused.

"You know what I mean. You're safe. I'm not ready to jump headfirst into the dating pool."

"I see."

"Don't feel hurt. I meant it in a good way."

Finally, he smiled and nodded slowly. "Abby said she wants us to get married. I told her you and I are just friends, but she didn't accept that."

"But I'm already married," Suzannah said, then realized what she'd said. "I mean, I was..."

Zach looked as uncomfortable as she felt. Why would Abby tell him that her Christmas wish was for her mother and him to get married?

"Zach, I'm so sorry. I don't know what to say."

He patted her shoulder. "Suzannah, don't let this upset you. I just wanted to tell you in case Abby doesn't tell you. She promised me she would, but I'm not sure she will. I think you two should talk."

"She promised if we went on one date, she'd stop bugging me about dating. Want to go out to dinner and put a stop to this nonsense?" Suzannah blurted.

"I don't know if we should feed this fire, do you?"

"No, no, of course not. I was teasing." She pushed her hair from her forehead. "I'm so sorry."

"Suzannah, you have no reason to be sorry."

She waved her hands. "I'm sorry about all of it. I've taken advantage of you for years, and now Abby thinks there's something more between us than friendship."

He surprised her by smiling slowly.

That smile got to her and quickened her pulse.

"Ah, Suzannah, but there *is* something between us," he said. "You know how much you mean to me."

She returned his smile. She knew. Zach was the best friend she'd ever had. She loved him deeply, but not in the way her daughter meant. She was going to have to talk to Abby soon.

"I'll talk to her this evening," she told Zach. "We'll squash this before it turns into a mess."

"Or as you said, we could grab that dinner, get her off our case, and go back to the way things were before she got a bee in her bonnet over this," he said.

"What about not feeding the fire?"

He pulled his mouth to one side. "Sometimes you have to fight fire with fire."

She paused a minute, studying his face. "Okay."

"Okay?"

"Let's do this." She met Zach's gaze and held it for a few seconds.

"For real."

"Sure. It's just a meal, right."

"Right."

"When?" she asked, feeling her pulse quicken even faster. "Where?"

"We'll work out the details later." With another small smile, he plucked his cowboy hat from the hat rack beside the door and headed out to his truck.

"All rightee then."

"Tell Abby I'll drive her home." He called over his shoulder. "I'll be waiting in the truck."

Suzannah turned and headed back inside the exam room. This day had taken a really strange turn, and she honestly wasn't sure how she felt about it.

Not in the least.

5

A few minutes later, Abby came out of the clinic, carrying Betty, and climbed into the back seat of his extended cab pickup truck.

"You ready?"

"Yep. Take us home, please."

"At your service," he said and drove from the parking lot. He looked at Abby in the rear-view mirror, she was rocking Betty in her arms as if she was a baby doll.

He drove through downtown Kringle, past the decorated Christmas displays and the courthouse square. "I talked to your mom."

A big grin crossed her face. "About you asking her to marry you?"

"Yes."

"Awesome sauce," Abby crowed. "So when are you getting married? I want to be in the wedding, and I don't mean as a flower girl. I'm too old to be—"

"Whoa, whoa." Zach frowned. Okay, that hadn't worked out right. "Slow down."

"What is it? Am I talking too fast?"

"No, we're *not* getting married, Abby. Your mom and I are just friends. I talked to her because I wanted her to know that you were hoping for something that won't happen. We'll go on a date as friends to please you, but that's all."

"Why can't it happen?" Abby looked hurt. "Why *can't* you get married?"

"That's why you need to talk to your mother. So she can explain."

"I don't get it. You like Mom. Mom likes you. *I* like you. You'd be a great dad."

"Sweetheart, it's not that simple. Your mom and dad were deeply in love. She'll love no man the same way she loved him." A deep ache caught him in the middle of his stomach, blindsiding Zach. He knew in his heart it was true.

There. That was the reason he and Suzannah could never be more than friends. She was still in love with Keith. Even death couldn't break that emotional bond. Keith was her first love and her last. Zach wondered what it would be like to have a woman love him the way Suzannah loved his best friend.

Abby notched up her chin. "I miss Dad too, but I know he's not coming back." Her voice caught, and she wiped at her eyes with her sleeve. Betty had fallen asleep in her lap. "Mom needs to move on. Everyone says so."

"Everyone being your friend Stephie?" Zach asked.

"And Grandma."

"I see." He pulled up in front of the small brick house where Suzannah and Abby lived. "Why don't you let your mother decide what's best for her?"

"Thanks for the ride," Abby said, cutting him off. She opened her door and hopped out. Then she picked up Betty and set her down in the driveway. Rather than pulling at the leash and trying to get away, Betty just cowered.

"C'mon Betty," Abby said, tugging on the leash.

Betty didn't move.

Helplessly, Abby met Zach's gaze. "What do I do now?"

Zach got out and hunkered down next to the dog and waved for Abby to crouch down too. "You need to realize that Betty has been through something traumatic."

"What happened to her?"

"We'll never know for sure, but dogs don't act this scared unless something bad happened. She needs time to adjust to you."

"How much time?" Abby looked worried.

"However long it takes."

Abby nibbled her bottom lip and looked forlorn. "Will she ever love me?"

"Yes, but it won't happen overnight. She's got to learn to trust you. Your job is important. You need to show her that she's safe and loved. Be patient and don't rush her to do things on your time schedule."

Abby nodded, and then she said, "And I need to do the same with Mom, right?"

Zach hadn't meant the discussion to have a double meaning, but now that he considered what he'd said, it definitely did. "Yes. You need to be patient."

Before he could add anything else, the front door opened, and Edith came out. He hadn't realized that Keith's mother was visiting since her car wasn't in the driveway.

"Hi, Edith." He stood and smiled at her.

"Zach." Her smile was tight, and her nod, while not exactly unfriendly, wasn't warm and inviting. Edith had made it clear over the years after Keith had died that she disapproved of his involvement with Suzannah and Abby. He wasn't exactly sure why.

"Grandma, look at the dog I adopted. Her name is Betty." Abby picked the dog up and cradled her to her chest.

Edith looked horrified. "You adopted a *dog?*" Glaring at Zach, she added, "Abby, you should have asked your mother first. Zach can't make this decision for your family."

"Mom said I could," Abby said. "We talked it over last night. It was her idea for Zach to take me."

Edith's immediate reaction might have hurt his feelings if it weren't for the empathy he felt for Keith's mother. Edith still struggled with the loss of her only child, and he knew that every time she saw him, she wondered why Zach was here and her son was not.

Edith patted the dog, then muttered, "Oh, okay. If your mother said you could have her."

Abby carried Betty into the house.

"Edith," Zach said, wanting to speak to her, but the older woman turned and walked inside.

With a sigh, he reminded himself of what he'd just told Abby. Patience. He needed to have patience. He knew Edith didn't really dislike him. She just found him to be a reminder of all she'd lost. When Keith had been alive, they'd been close friends who hung out a lot and Edith had been nice to him back then.

Patience. He needed to give her time.

He gathered the dog medication and food Dr. Chloe had given Abby at the animal clinic and took them inside the house. He couldn't do anything about Edith's feelings, but he could help Betty get the love she deserved.

The next morning over oatmeal, Abby made an announcement, "I know you and Zach said you won't fall in love and get married, but you said you'd go on a date, so I thought I'd help. I made a reservation for you at Pierre's tonight at eight."

"What?" Stunned, Suzannah stared at her daughter. The kid was ten going on thirty. "When did you do that?"

"Just now." Abby held up her phone and showed her mother the Open Table app.

"Pierre's is the most expensive restaurant in Kringle," Suzannah said. "I'm not suggesting it to Zach."

"It's also the nicest restaurant in Kringle," Abby said. "I know that's where Zach would want to take you."

"You're overstepping your bounds, young lady. Please cancel that reservation."

"But you promised you'd go on a date."

"I said I would think about it."

Abby hung her head. "I was just trying to help. All I want is to see you happy."

"I know, sweetheart." Suzannah softened her tone.

"So you'll go?" Abby's voice lifted.

"You're relentless." Suzannah chuckled and shook her head.

"So—"

"I'll talk to Zach and see if he's free tonight."

"He is. I already texted him."

Suzannah frowned. "Abby, if I go on a date with Zach, it's up to him and me. Got it, young lady?"

"Yes, ma'am."

Shaking her head, Suzannah got up and went to the other side of the kitchen table. She kissed her daughter on the top of her head and gave her a big hug. "I know you just want the best for me."

"I do," Abby said, tears shining in her eyes.

"You better scoot or you're going to be late for school. Did you feed Betty this morning?"

"Yes, ma'am."

"And took her out to potty?"

"Uh-huh."

"Good job."

"I'm glad you get to take her to work with you," Abby said. "I'd hate for her to stay home alone all day."

"We are lucky to have doggy day care at the Kringle Animal Clinic." Suzannah glanced out the window. "Looks like your ride is here."

Abby polished off her last bite of oatmeal and picked up her backpack just as their neighbor stopped her carpool van in the driveway. "Bye, Mom."

"Have a great day, sweetheart." She gave Abby another hug and sent her out the door. She stood on the front porch waving goodbye.

How could she stay mad at her daughter who wanted nothing more than to see her mother happy? Maybe Abby had gone about it the wrong way, but she'd had the best intentions.

Suzannah loaded their breakfast dishes into the dishwasher and got dressed in the burgundy scrubs she wore to work at the vet clinic. She went to Abby's bedroom and found Betty curled up in the middle of Abby's bed.

Betty looked up at her with guilty eyes and crawled down off the bed.

"Hey, it's okay to sleep on the bed in this house," Suzannah squatted to pet the dog. "No need to feel guilty."

The little dog licked the back of Suzannah's hand. Aww, she was so precious. Suzannah pulled her cell phone out of her pocket to check the time. Her shift started at eight and it was seven-thirty. The clinic was only two miles from her house. She had time to call Zach and tell him what her matchmaking daughter had done.

With a sigh, she hit Zach's number on her speed dial.

"Morning, Suzie-Q," Zach said, using her high school nickname. Only one other person had ever called her that and he was no longer alive. "What's up?"

The sound of his deep voice brought a warm, soft feeling to her heart. "You won't believe this."

"What's Abby up to now?"

"How did you know?"

"That girl is a firecracker." He laughed.

"My daughter made dinner reservations for us at Pierre's tonight at eight."

"She did what?"

"I am so sorry. I've lost control as a mother."

"You haven't," he said. "Abby's just a headstrong girl who knows her own mind. You should be proud of her."

"I am, it's just she's really hung up on this idea of us dating."

"She just wants to see you happy."

"I *am* happy..."

"But?"

Why had she hesitated? "Maybe I do get a little lonely sometimes. But hey, that's what Betty is for, right?"

Betty seemed to agree, she'd curled up on Suzannah's shoes and gone back to sleep.

She wasn't sure why she didn't automatically cancel the reservation and not even bother calling Zach, but she felt compelled to talk to him about this.

He was silent for a moment, and she waited anxiously for his response. She didn't know why she suddenly felt this way, but ever since Abby had brought up the subject, Suzannah had felt that maybe she should move on, at least a little.

She spun her engagement and wedding rings. She was still wearing them when it had been three years but removing them didn't seem right. Now, however, they were a symbol of what was holding her back. Clinging to a love long gone.

"Zach?" she said when he still had said nothing. "I should cancel the dinner reservation, right?"

What was wrong with her? She knew the answer. She should cancel the reservation.

So why hadn't she?

"No, don't cancel. Let's have dinner. It will be fun," he said. "We could both use a night out."

She wasn't sure this was a good idea. In fact, she was fairly certain it was a terrible idea.

But then why hadn't she simply canceled the reservation? Equally important, why wasn't Zach telling her to cancel it?

"I think we've both lost our minds," she said with a light laugh. "Do you think by going to dinner we're getting Abby's hopes up? We shouldn't lead her to believe this will turn into anything."

He didn't respond right away, and Suzannah wished she could see his face. Zach had always been such an important part of her life, especially since Keith's death, that she couldn't help wondering how he really felt about Abby's shenanigans.

"Zach?" she asked.

Finally, he said, "We'll make it clear to Abby that this is just two friends having dinner."

"I could tell her it's a test date. Go out without someone I trust before I risk dipping my toe into the dating pool."

"You could," he said, but the tone in his voice suggested he didn't love being a test date. "I'll pick you up at seven-thirty if that's okay."

"That's fine. I'll see you then." She hung up, and suddenly, she felt like she was a teenager again, about to go on a date with the cutest boy in class. She knew it was silly. She and Zach had dinner together often. Sure, it was always with Abby, but tonight's dinner wasn't anything special. It was simply two friends enjoying a meal together.

So if it was no big deal, why couldn't she get the butterflies in her stomach to settle down?

Suzannah looked down at her rings once more. She wouldn't feel right wearing them on a date but taking them off signaled something monumental.

Was she ready to do it?

Betty whimpered as if picking up on her mood. Suzannah stared down at the little dog who thumped her tail and rolled over for a belly scratch.

Face it. Things were changing around here. It was time for her to accept that and finally move on. Not with Zach necessarily, but with her life.

Slowly, hesitantly, Suzannah took off her rings and with sadness in her heart, tucked them into her jewelry box. "I'll always love you, Keith," she whispered. "But it's time to let you go."

6

Zach pulled into Suzannah's driveway and wondered for the millionth time if he'd lost his ever-loving mind. That was the only explanation. Suzannah mentioned they both might be a little crazy, and boy, was she right. Getting involved with her romantically threatened to destroy the friendship they'd built over the last decade.

Over the course of the day, he'd almost called her a dozen times to cancel, but each time, something stopped him, because he couldn't get his mind off what Abby had said.

Abby firmly believed he and Suzannah belonged together.

Yes, she was a precocious ten-year-old with a tendency to stick her nose in where it didn't belong. She was an earnest kid with a heart the size of Texas and Zach loved her for it.

And he was thinking Abby had a point. He cared

about Suzannah. He had cared about her long before she'd married Keith. His feelings for her had only deepened during the last three years.

So was this step a mistake, or the best chance he'd ever have?

He opened the door to his truck and climbed out. Taking a deep breath, he headed toward the front door decorated with a huge Christmas wreath. He'd dressed up for this dinner in a suit and tie, and now he felt uncomfortable in more ways than one.

Abby threw open the front door before he had time to knock. "You look sooo handsome."

She had Betty tucked into the crook of her elbow. The little dog looked bright-eyed and perky. She wagged her tail and didn't tremble at all.

"Mom!" Abby hollered. "Zach is here!"

Abby held up Betty. "Doesn't she look nice? I gave her a bath and brushed her fur. She also has a new collar, see?" She turned Betty showing off her red collar.

Zach patted Betty. "She looks beautiful."

More than pretty, the dog looked happy. Abby placed her on the ground and the two ran off toward the back of the house. They disappeared into the kitchen, and Edith wandered into the foyer.

"Hello, Zach," she said.

He might not be the smartest cowboy in town, but he was smart enough to pick up on her tone. Edith was not happy.

"Hi, Edith. How are you tonight?" He flashed his

best smile, but it did nothing to soften the frown on her face.

"Abby keeps saying you and Suzannah are going on a date, but I told her that can't be right," she said.

Although she didn't say it aloud, Zach knew what she was thinking. *How could he do this to Keith?* He'd thought the same thing for a long, long time. But three years had passed since Keith's death. He missed his buddy, but life had to go on.

"It's just a dinner, Edith," he said. "It's not a big deal."

"That's true," Suzannah said from behind him.

Zach turned and immediately felt the air leave his lungs. She, too, had dressed up for dinner. She had on a beautiful dark blue dress that made her eyes seem even bluer and hugged her curves. Her long blonde hair was loose around her shoulders and glistened in the hallway lighting. She wore heels. Not too high, but tall enough to show off her shapely legs.

Dumbstruck, Zach stuttered, "Y-You look g-gorgeous."

She rewarded him with a small smile and her cheeks pinked. She dropped her gaze, murmured, "You look very nice too."

Zach wanted to say more, but he knew Edith was glaring at them. He could feel her disapproval washing over him.

"Thank you for watching Abby," Suzannah said to Edith. "It's very nice of you."

"I don't mind. Although I'm not sure about that dog."

"Abby loves her so much. They will be so good for each other."

"I really think you should have thought about this longer before you let her get a dog."

"I've been thinking about it for a while, Edith. This wasn't impulsive."

"First, I've heard of it."

"I don't have to run all my decisions by you," Suzannah said kindly yet firmly. "Just as you don't have to run your decisions by me."

"I've never liked pets," Edith muttered. "They make messes."

"Abby will clean up any messes Betty makes," Suzannah said. "Don't worry."

Zach headed over to the front door. He knew how Edith felt about pets. For years when they'd been teens, Keith had begged his mother to let him have a dog, but she wouldn't allow it.

Suzannah picked up her purse and walked over to join Zach by the door. And that's when he saw that she'd taken off her wedding and engagement rings.

His heart rate kicked up, and he tried to ignore it but darn he if he could. Why had she taken off her rings now when she'd been wearing them for three years after her husband died? Why on the night of their first date? Was it because Suzannah might think they could be more than friends?

He didn't dare hope.

"You won't be home late," Edith said as they headed out the door. She wasn't asking a question. She'd made a very firm statement.

"No, we won't be home late," Suzannah agreed.

Zach closed the front door behind them, deliberately not making any promises he couldn't keep.

She felt like she was cheating.

That's all Suzannah could think as she studied the menu at Pierre's and rubbed the back of her bare ring finger with her thumb. She knew it was silly, but she couldn't help feeling like she was betraying Keith by going on a date with his best friend.

"What looks good to you?" Zach asked.

You do, she almost said, then caught herself at the last moment. *Yikes. She was a mess*. This change in her relationship with Zach was really throwing her. She wasn't ready to move on, wasn't ready to get involved in a romance with anyone. Taking off the rings had meant to signal that she was ready, but when the rubber met the road, she was not.

And yet, her body thought otherwise.

Every time he smiled at her or touched her, she tingled from head to toe and her stomach pitched, and her pulse sped up. She felt both excited and guilty.

How crazy was that?

"I don't know what to do." She stared at the

menu, not really seeing the food options. She was just too aware of *him*.

He must have understood because he set his menu down and looked at her. "There's nothing to do but have a nice meal."

"It just feels so...I don't know...backwards."

"What do you mean?"

"We're as close as two friends can be, Zach. We know everything there is to know about each other. I remember where you got that scar..." She nodded at the deep nick on his arm just above his wrist. "You and Keith were roping and heeling longhorns and one of them got you good."

"No kidding." Zach rubbed the scar at his wrist.

"I know your favorite color is blue, that you love baseball better than football, but you don't want anyone to know because it feels unTexan. That you like your steaks medium rare and your whiskey neat, but you hardly ever drink. That you prefer Chevys over Fords and cashews to peanuts. That you can't stand reality TV because there is nothing real about it. You love country music and Shania Twain is your favorite artist, but you also have a secret fondness for rockabilly." She paused and waved a hand. "And you know me just as well. What are we going to talk about on this date?"

Zach nodded. "I thought it was a crazy idea when Abby brought it up, but after I've thought about it, it doesn't seem so crazy."

His words caught her off guard. For a moment,

she sat still, unsure what to say and overcome by so many feelings that she truly had no words. Finally, all she managed was, "Zach."

His gaze never waived from hers. "I know. It seems strange, but I've been thinking about it. You and I spend almost every day together. You're the first person I call when something good—or something bad—happens."

She nodded because she did the same. Whenever something unusual happened to her, she called Zach. She shared her day with him, and she looked forward to hearing about his.

But was that enough?

"But that isn't a romance, Zach."

He nodded slowly. "Not by itself. But maybe it's something to build on. Being close friends is a heck of a start."

The waiter appeared with bread, and that gave her time to gather her thoughts. Zach ordered a steak medium rare and Suzannah picked the mushroom risotto.

Unfurling her napkin in her lap, Suzannah considered what he'd said. Was being really good friends enough to build on a romantic relationship on?

She'd heard people say they were friends before they fell in love, but she'd never experienced that. She and Keith fell in love almost immediately. They weren't friends who later developed a romance. They'd fallen in love and stayed in love. There had been fireworks and loads of chemistry.

But with Zach things were steadier, quieter. No rockets. No sweaty palms. No jitteriness. No roller-coaster of emotions. She knew she could count on him and he would always be there for her, no matter what.

When the waiter walked away, Zach said, "Why don't we just take things slow? We can just spend some time together. We can call it a date or not. We can just call it friends spending time together. We don't have to decide right now."

What he was saying made sense. They could simply spend time together and see where it led. Still, she had concerns. "What if dating destroys our friendship?"

Zach chuckled, the sound deep and comforting. "Suzannah, you and I have been through way too much for anything to destroy our friendship."

She smiled. She'd like to think that. She'd like to believe that their friendship could survive anything.

Still, she wasn't sure if she was ready for this step. Dating Zach meant shifting gears and seeing him in a different light. "You have a good point, but I'm not sure I can do this. I feel guilty and confused. I keep thinking of Keith..."

Rather than dismissing her feelings, Zach nodded. "I understand. I don't want you to feel that I'm pressuring you, because I'm not. I enjoy being around you and I think you enjoy being around me. But the ball is in your court."

"I do enjoy being around you." She smiled. As always, Zach cared about others.

"Maybe you should date someone less complicated," she said, knowing in her heart that she would hate that but also knowing it wasn't fair to Zach to let him think things with her could turn romantic when they might not.

He shook his head and flashed her his famous grin. "Now why would I want to do a crazy thing like that? I love complicated."

Good thing, Suzannah decided as the waiter brought their meals, because dating would definitely get complicated.

Dejected, Zach held the door for Suzannah to climb into the passenger seat of his truck and then he headed around to the driver's side, shaking his head.

A blizzard could hit Kringle and close all the roads and still not be as much as a disaster as dinner with Suzannah had turned out to be. Several times during the dinner, he had tried to make her feel comfortable, but it soon became obvious it wasn't really working.

Both of them had acted so goofy. He knew she felt guilty about Keith. He also knew his buddy would have wanted Suzannah to move on and build a new life. Dinner had been awkward and uncomfortable. He couldn't remember ever feeling that way around Suzannah.

"Thanks for joining me for dinner," he said when he settled into the driver's seat. "It was nice."

She surprised him by bursting into laughter. "No, it wasn't. It was terrible. I felt nervous and jumpy throughout the whole meal. I kept blathering on about the Christmas parade and our Santa and Mrs. Claus costumes."

Zach laughed too, relieved that she had felt as uncomfortable as he had. "Hey, I wasn't much better. I think I spent twenty minutes explaining how I repair broken fencing on my ranch."

They drove in silence for a few minutes. Normally, sitting silently with Suzannah wasn't uncomfortable. They had been friends for so many years that they didn't feel the need to talk constantly.

But tonight, the silence was beyond uncomfortable. It felt like a living thing, sitting between them in the truck.

Finally, Zach said, "I have to be honest, Suzannah. I don't want to go back to just being friends. So, here's an idea. Let's just not put a label on this. We aren't dating. We aren't just friends. We aren't..." He shrugged, knowing full well that she couldn't see it in the dark. "We're just us."

She said nothing.

His chest twisted tight. Tension constricted his spine. Ah heck, he'd blown it. He quelled the impulse to tell her to scratch that. He didn't mean it. He'd lost his mind. But he meant it.

"Given how tonight went..." She paused.

Fear clogged his throat, terrified she was going to tell him she could no longer be friends with him. He gripped the steering wheel tighter and cursed himself for pushing things too far.

"I don't think we can be anything other than *us*."

He held his breath and shot a sidelong glance her way. What did she mean by that? "We're still friends?"

"Zach," she said. "You'll always be my friend. I can't imagine my life without you in it."

He relaxed his grip on the steering wheel. At least he hadn't messed that up.

"As far as anything more, let's just take it one day at a time."

Hope fluttered in his chest. She hadn't completely shut the door on romance. Hope was encouraging, yes, but he couldn't remember ever being as confused about anything in his life as he was about this relationship with Suzannah.

Until Abby had suggested that he marry her mother, he hadn't really thought about anything more between them. At least, not really. He respected his late friend too much to make a move on his wife, and he hadn't wanted to blow his friendship with Suzannah.

But ever since Abby put the idea in his head, it was the only thing he could think about. Personally, he agreed with Abby. He really thought he and Suzannah would be perfect together. They got along so well. Had never had a fight. A few differences of opinions sure, but nothing they couldn't work through.

They enjoyed many of the same things—small-town life, feel-good movies, riding horses, hanging out with Abby. They had the same values—they believed in family, honor and doing the right thing. They had a shared history reaching back to high school.

And that was the problem.

Their shared history.

Keith.

Her late husband, and his best friend, was the obstacle between them. How could he compete with a dead man?

Zach pulled up in front of Suzannah's house and turned off the truck. Moved to get out so he could walk her to the door, but before he could wrench the door open, she placed one hand on his arm.

"Wait. Before we go in, I just wanted to thank you for tonight."

Confused, he asked, "I'm not sure you should thank me. I'm not sure it turned out that great."

She laughed softly. "Yes, it did. Tonight was the first time since Keith died that I've tried even a little to move on. I couldn't have done it if you hadn't been there with me. So, thank you."

"I'm not really sure what to say."

She laughed again. "I know, right? I couldn't have gone on a date without my best friend. It makes no sense. You're my closest friend, the person who is always there for me, and I would have been too nervous and upset to go on this date with anyone else. I know it shows how much you mean to me, but I also realize it shows how important your friendship is. I worry that I will lose that, but I'm going to be brave and try."

He started to respond, but before he could, she stunned him by leaning forward and kissing him.

Nothing could have surprised Zach more, and for a moment, he didn't respond, unable to believe this was really happening.

Suzannah was kissing *him?*

His heart pounded, and he broke out in a cold sweat. What should he do?

But the feel of her lips on his eradicated all rational thought. Desire raced through his body, and he gathered her close.

Zach deepened the kiss but let her set the pace, holding her loosely in case she wanted to pull away. His nose filled with the delightful smell of her, and his pulse quickened. Finally, finally, at last, he was kissing Suzannah. He'd dreamed of this for twenty years.

For a few moments, they kissed in silence, then she finally broke the connection. Zach could have gone on kissing until the end of time.

"Wow," she whispered and fingered her lips. "Wow. You sure can kiss, Zach Delaney."

He chuckled. "Thank you, ma'am. You sure can kiss, too."

They stared at each other, eyes locked and a fresh silence descended over the cab of his truck.

He wasn't sure what else to say and was more than a little relieved when she pushed open her door. He climbed out of the truck and walked her to the front door. Wracking his brain for something to say, but for the life of him, he came up empty.

Thankfully, Abby threw open the front door, a wide grin on her face and Betty in her arms, saving him from the conversation.

"You're home! Did you have fun? Was it romantic? Are you in love?" She rattled off the questions so fast Zach couldn't keep track of them all. He figured he'd best let Suzannah handle her daughter.

"Yes, we're home. Yes, we had fun. Yes, it was romantic, and we care about each other a great deal," she said. Then she lightly tapped the end of her daughter's nose. "You need to keep your nose out of other people's business."

Rather than being discouraged, Abby's grin just grew wider. "Sure. I'll butt out. I'll let you two handle this on your own." She grinned at her dog. "I'll be good, and so will Betty."

With that, she turned and headed back inside, laughing as she went.

Suzannah sighed. "Why do I have a feeling she didn't mean that promise?"

Zach nodded slowly. "Because this isn't your first rodeo."

"I had a nice time," she said, but Edith called from the kitchen, cutting her short.

"Suzannah? Is that you? Is the date over?" Edith asked.

"I guess I'd better go," she murmured and smiled at him.

He nodded and wished her good night. Then he headed back to his truck feeling like a Texas twister had just smacked into him. Confused about the best way to handle this situation, he climbed inside his truck, dazed and dazzled. After their kiss, he was sure of one thing.

He wanted to marry his best friend.

7

Inside the house, Suzannah leaned against the door, catching her breath and orienting herself to the here and now before facing her mother-in-law.

She fingered her lips, still tingling from Zach's kiss, and ducked her head to hide the wide grin spreading across her face, just in case Edith came into the foyer and asked her what was so amusing.

Feeling giddy with the taste of Zach still on her tongue, she wanted to throw back her head and laugh out loud.

"Suzannah?" Edith called again from the kitchen where Abby had gone.

"Be right there," she said, putting on her game face, and strolled into the kitchen.

She found Edith and Abby sitting at the kitchen table, a bowl of popcorn and an open photo album in front of them. Suzannah strolled over, trying hard to act casual and grabbed a handful of popcorn and took a bite.

"Hmm, kettle corn. Did you make this?"

Edith wrinkled her nose. "We cheated and got the packaged stuff."

"Good brand, though. Tasty." Munching, Suzannah bent over to see which album they'd dug out. She was really good about keeping her photo albums organized and up to date. Or at least she had been before Keith died.

It was the album from eleven years ago. The year before Abby was born. The page flipped open to the back of the album. Christmas. When Suzannah had shared the delightful news with Keith that she was finally pregnant.

A knot of tears clotted her throat, but she swallowed them back.

"You and Dad look so young." Abby traced a finger over the clear plastic sleeve protecting the photograph.

"We *were* young." Suzannah sat in the chair beside her daughter and leaned over her shoulder. "There's the ornament I put on the tree to let your father know he was about to become a Daddy."

"I know, I know." Abby rolled her eyes. "The stork delivering a baby in a pink blanket ornament. You tell me that story every year when we decorate the Christmas tree. *Corn-ee.*"

"Hey," Suzannah cupped her daughter's chin in her palm, gently forced her to look into her face.

"The day we knew we were having you was the happiest day of our lives. Don't roll your eyes at it. You are our greatest blessing."

"Amen to that young lady," Edith added.

"Yes, ma'am." Abby lowered her lashes, contrite.

Suzannah leaned over to kiss her forehead. "You are the most precious thing to me in the world and don't you ever forget it."

"Aww, Mom, don't get mushy." Abby rubbed her forehead.

"You let your mom love on you all she wants, Abigail Marie," Edith chided. "I'd give anything in the world just to hug my boy one more time."

"Me too," Suzannah whispered. "Now scoot off to bed, doodle bug."

Abby jumped up and hugged first her mom and then her grandmother. "Night, night, Gramma."

Once Abby had zipped out of the room, Suzannah met Edith's gaze. Shared sorrow, that great equalizer, linked them. Tears misted Edith's eyes, and she turned her head. To be kind, Suzannah locked her attention on the photo album.

Her gaze fell on a photograph of her and Keith having a snowball fight. She remembered that Chloe, back before she'd become a doctor, had snapped the picture.

Pink-cheeked and laughing, Suzannah had her head thrown back and Keith was popping up to lob a snowball at her from behind their Camry. In the foreground was a snowman they'd just finished building and in the background, the front porch of this very house.

On the porch lounged Zach, and he was looking at Suzannah with such stark longing on his face that she sucked in her breath.

She'd seen this picture hundreds of times and had never noticed Zach's gaze fixed on her. Her heart skipped a beat, and she stopped breathing entirely. How long had Zach felt something more than friendship toward her?

"Suzannah?"

She blinked and glanced up at Edith, who'd stood up and had her purse in her hand. "Yes?"

"When did you stop wearing your wedding rings?"

"I—"

"It was tonight, wasn't it? Because you went out with *him*."

"It wasn't because of Zach," Suzannah assured her. "It was time."

Tears formed in Edith's eyes, and she whispered, "I know."

That surprised her. She'd expected her mother-in-law to put up a fuss about the rings.

"You wore yours a lot longer than I wore mine after Keith's father died."

"Oh," she said.

"You're much braver than I ever was," Edith said.

Wow. "Thank you for saying that."

"I'm going to head home now," Edith said.

"It's late," Suzannah invited, unsure if she felt

relieved or disappointment that Edith was cutting their touching conversation short. "You're welcome to stay the night."

"That's sweet of you, dear." She patted Suzannah's hand. "But I want to sleep in my bed."

"Well, thank you for sitting with Abby."

"It's always my pleasure."

Suzannah grabbed her jacket and walked Edith out to her car. "Drive safely," she said, hugging herself against the cold night air.

"I know I sound like a sentimental old fool," Edith said, with her window down. "But thank you for letting me part of your life. You could have shut me out. Many daughters-in-law's might have shut me out, but you didn't."

"You're Abby's grandmother. I could never do that to either of you."

"I can be a pill sometimes, I know that, but I appreciate your patience with me."

Suzannah reached in through the window and squeezed Edith's hand. "Sleep well."

With her bottom lip trembling, Edith gave her a feeble smile. "I know Zach is your good friend, but I'm uncertain he's the right man for you."

"Thank you for your input," Suzannah said, letting go of Edith's hand and stepping away from the car.

"He's a nice young man, but he's thirty-five and never married. Ask yourself why? What's wrong with him?"

You're jealous, Suzannah thought, *because he's alive*

and Keith isn't. "Goodnight, Edith," she said kindly, then turned and walked back into the house.

Wandering back into the kitchen, she sat back down at the table, opened the photo album that Abby had closed earlier, flipped to the back and found the picture of the snowball fight.

And studied Zach's face as he looked at her. No mistaking the yearning on his handsome face. The song, "Jesse's Girl" popped into her head. Had he been pining for her all these years?

Why *hadn't* he ever married? He was good looking, financially set, a hard worker, kind and considerate. He'd dated, but nothing had stuck. Why not?

Was the answer to that question staring right at her?

The following Saturday, Suzannah invited Zach to join her and Abby while they made their annual Christmas cookies with some of their friends from town. Abby's friend Stephie and Edith always joined them, but other people came as well.

Normally baking Christmas cookies with friends was a high point of the holiday season, but this year, with the addition of Zach, she couldn't help feeling awkward. Especially after she'd seen that old photograph.

She'd sent him a quick text the day before, half hoping he'd say he had other plans, but within seconds, he'd texted back saying he'd love to be there.

As she set out the ingredients and listened to her daughter tell her best friend all about Betty's latest adventures, Suzannah made her own Christmas wish that Edith would be kind to Zach.

Her mother-in-law made it clear every time she'd seen Suzannah that she questioned her changing relationship with Zach.

But as more time passed, the less Suzannah cared. She didn't want to hurt Edith, but, she couldn't stay stuck in the past. Moving forward didn't mean she didn't love Keith. She had, and she still did.

She had complicated feelings where Zach was concerned, and she still didn't know where things would go with them, but she knew one thing. She needed to live in the present, not the past. Not just for herself, but also for her daughter.

She had just finished setting out all the supplies when the backdoor opened and Edith came in without knocking, as was her usual habit. When Keith was alive, she had come to the front door and rang the doorbell. But after he died, she had just started using her key and coming in whenever she felt like it.

A few times over the last couple of years, Suzannah had thought about asking her not to just walk in, but she hadn't spoken up. She knew that Edith thought it was her right as Abby's grandmother, but she and Abby would never dream of simply walking into Edith's house. They always knocked on the door.

Perhaps it was time to set some boundaries with her mother-in-law. Suzannah was still considering how to bring it up with Edith when Abby bounced into the room.

"Grandma, let us know you're coming in now that we have Betty," Abby said, scurrying around her grandmother to grab Betty before she dashed out the door. "Just ring the bell and we'll put her up first."

Well, look at that. Abby had handled the situation for her.

Edith looked down Betty and wrinkled her nose. "I have to change because of a dog?"

Abby shrugged. "We all have to make adjustments. Betty is part of the family, and we have to be sure to keep her safe."

Edith's eyes narrowed and her mouth thinned. "She's a dog. I'm a person."

Abby nodded and ran over to hug her grandmother. "You're a person, which is why you know how important it is to be kind to animals like Betty. She needs you to help take care of her, Gramma. Just knock on the front door, and I'll put Betty in my room and then you can come in. Easy-peasy."

When Edith still seemed to waver, Abby gave her a big hug and a smacking kiss on her cheek. "You're the best gramma in the world."

That sealed the deal. Edith sighed and then flashed a weak smile at Suzannah. "Guess I'll knock from now on," she said. "I hope you don't mind, dear."

"Not at all. I think it's wisest." The change in protocol delighted Suzannah and especially delighted that it had happened in such a way as to not offend Edith. The woman was always welcome in their home, but it was only polite to knock before entering.

She was also very proud of her daughter. Abby had handled the situation in a way that Edith's feelings didn't appear to be too hurt. She was now sitting with Abby and Stephie and watching as they tried to teach Betty how to sit on command. The two girls weren't having much luck, so Edith offered a few suggestions.

Watching them made her happy. She was glad that Edith was part of their lives, and she always would be. No matter what happened with Zach, that much would never change. Edith was Abby's grandmother and that would never change.

When the doorbell rang, Suzannah hurried to open it.

Zach came in carrying supplies for Betty. Before she could say more than just hi, two of her neighbors stopped by. For the next half an hour, Suzannah was busy getting everyone set with cookies to decorate.

Because she was too busy to talk, she paired Zach with Edith. Maybe they could bond.

"Edith, will you help Zach get started?" She flashed a smiled at both of them.

Zach rewarded her with one of his lopsided grins. He'd flashed that grin at her countless times over the years, but today, it made her pulse pick up and that flustered her.

Edith looked from Suzannah to Zach and back again, narrowed her eyes and pursed her lips.

"I'm sure Zach can do this by himself. I'll go help someone else," Edith said and walked away from him.

Zach came to stand beside Suzannah. "She's not happy," he murmured. "Maybe I should go talk to her?"

Suzannah drew in a deep breath. "No. Leave her be. Let's just give her time."

Edith perched near Abby and Stephie. Suzannah went around the room to make sure everyone had what they needed, then she settled next to Zach at the other end of the table from Edith and the girls and together they started decorating cookies.

As they worked, she and Zach laughed and joked, seeing which one could create the most outrageous Christmas cookie. Zach made a snowman with a nose so long it reached to his chest. Suzannah one-upped him by using a big glob of black icing to fashion a pork-pie hat on Rudolph's head.

"I remember when Keith was little," Edith said loudly, cutting into their conversation. "Keith *loved* Christmas cookies, and he loved George Strait's song "Christmas Cookies." Do you remember how he'd put on that song when you were baking cookies, and waltz you around the kitchen, Suzannah?"

Suzannah stopped, a chill running across her skin. She looked at her mother-in-law.

Edith shot her a wily smiled and said, “He was such as a wonderful husband, wasn’t he, Suzannah?”

Suzannah knew what she was doing and why. Edith worried that Suzannah was forgetting about her son, but this approach was unfair. She glanced at Abby, worried that Edith’s words would hurt her, but Abby was giggling with Stephie and not paying her grandmother any attention.

Suzannah glanced at Zach.

He smiled and shook his head, forgiving Edith. The man had the patience of Job.

Suzannah couldn’t help feeling sorry for her mother-in-law. Losing Keith was hard on all of them, but Suzannah had to move on and the more time that passed, the more Suzannah was convinced that this was the right thing.

“Excuse me a moment,” she murmured to Zach.

She walked over to Edith intending on saying something a little sharp, nothing mean, just enough to set boundaries. But the grief-stricken expression on her mother-in-law’s face broke her heart.

Suzannah leaned forward and hugged her. “Keith was a wonderful husband, but he was terrible at cookie decorating.”

Edith hugged her back and then said. “Yes. Yes, he was. When he was a kid, I remember making him eat all the ones he decorated. They were too ugly to give to anyone else.”

Abby appeared next to them holding a cookie. “Apparently, I inherited his lack of cookie decorating skills.” She giggled and held up an awful cookie to show her point.

Suzannah and Edith laughed together.

Red and white blobs covered the cookie. “Do I have to eat all the cookies I decorated?” Abby asked hopefully.

“What in the world is that supposed to be?” Edith asked, inspecting the cookie from several angles.

“It’s supposed to be Zach in his Santa costume,” Abby said. She held up the cookie for Zach to see.

“Naw, that cookie looks better than I did in that costume,” Zach said.

Abby chortled. “No doubt.”

“I remember a certain young lady telling me I looked horrendous.”

“Terrible,” Abby corrected. “I said, you look *terrible.*”

“And that’s better?” Zach teased.

Abby skipped away, laughing and carrying her messy cookie.

Edith followed her granddaughter, throwing over her shoulder. “I’ll show her the right way to decorate.”

Once her daughter and mother-in-law settled and were happily decorating cookies again, Suzannah headed back to join Zach. She glanced down at the cookie in front of him.

"Seems like you inherited that bad cookie decorating gene too," she teased.

Zach had been looking at her, but then he glanced down at the mottled cookie in his hand. He held it up and inspected it with exaggerated slowness. As he studied the cookie, he kept saying to the cookie, "Don't let her shame you. You're an exquisite cookie."

His silliness made Suzannah laugh, and she felt her tension ease.

"Stop it. I wasn't bullying your cookie," she said, still laughing at his nonsense.

Zach held the cookie close and pretended to pat it. "Poor, Cookie. Everyone is so mean to you. Don't worry. I love you."

Then he took a huge bite out of the cookie and chewed happily. "You are truly wonderful."

Suzannah burst out laughing and felt a spontaneous hug rising in her, but she stopped herself before she hugged Zach.

Until last Friday, she would have hugged Zach and not thought a thing about it. But ever since their dinner together, everything had changed. Suddenly, the smallest gesture took on new and weighted meaning.

"You're not supposed to eat the cookies today," she told him with mock sternness.

"Arrest me," he said, then he held the half-eaten cookie in front of her. You should eat the rest," he said, his gaze meeting hers. "Help me commit this crime. We can go to cookie prison together."

Suzannah froze.

The way Zach was looking at her and the deep, quiet tone of his voice were getting to her. More than anything, she wanted to kiss him.

She took one small step toward him, and she could tell from his expression that he knew what she was thinking.

A small smile grew on his lips as she got closer.

Before she could do anything, though, Abby jumped between them.

"I'll go to cookie prison with you," she said, grabbing the remaining cookie and gobbling it down.

Abby's antics made everyone laugh. If Abby hadn't jumped in, Suzannah might have kissed Zach in front of her neighbors and friends.

And in front of Edith.

Suzannah couldn't help thinking that whether her daughter meant to do it or not, Abby had just saved her from making a big mistake.

⁂ 8 ⁂

In a moment of craziness, Zach had volunteered to help decorate the elementary school auditorium for the winter concert. Two weeks ago, the principle, Mike Lockwood, had coaxed him into it after Mike helped Zach round up some cattle that had gotten out.

Two weeks ago it seemed an easy enough task, but now that the day was here, Zach wasn't looking forward to it. He had so much else going on, a big part of which was figuring out his relationship with Suzannah.

He arrived at the school just as classes were letting out, parked and was getting his extension ladder from his truck—Mike had asked him to bring it since they were short on ladders—when Abby bebopped up to the tailgate.

"Hi."

"Hello."

"What are you doing here?" she asked.

"Helping decorate the auditorium."

"No, no, you've *got* to help with the float decorations."

"I'm already committed to this project," he pointed out. "I promised Principal Lockwood."

"I know, and we appreciate you, but we also need help with the float." She bounced along beside him as he carried the ladder toward the auditorium. When they got closer, she raced ahead to open the door for him.

"It's a busy time of year," she chattered as he walked past her into the auditorium, careful not to whack her with the ladder. "It's important to pitch in."

Zach wanted to tell her he was pitching in and then remind her that he had his own ranch to oversee, but the pitiful look Abby gave him tweaked his heart as it always did. He was putty in this kid's hands.

"Dang it, stop looking at me that way," he grumbled with a smile. Getting tapped to volunteer was all part of living in a close-knit community like Kringle.

Abby pressed her palms together, in front of her chest, begging. "Please, please, please."

"Okay, later this week I'll help with the float. Let's get ready for tonight's concert. I don't want any snowflakes I hang to fall and bonk some kiddo on the head mid-song."

Abby giggled. "It wouldn't hurt. The snowflakes are only paper."

"Doesn't matter. I still don't want it happening because I did sloppy work." Zach set up his ladder in the middle of the auditorium, located the box of snowflakes Principal Lockwood had tasked him with hanging from the ceiling, climbed up the ladder and started work.

He wasn't the only one working. Other adults were there decorating the stage, and he exchanged greetings with them. To Abby, he said, "Since you're standing there doing nothing, hand me the snowflakes as I'm ready to hang them."

"Okay."

For the next hour, Abby fed him snowflakes as he moved the ladder from spot to spot until finally, the ceiling lay covered with the festive white paper cutouts and it looked like a winter wonderland.

Satisfied with his handiwork, Zach closed up his ladder. "Come on," he said to Abby. "Let's get you home. Your mother will wonder where you are," he said.

"I already texted her."

"Good thinking."

"You know," Abby said as she climbed into the back seat of his truck. "You should take her out to dinner before the concert. That would be a really nice thing to do. Thoughtful and romantic and show Mom what a great guy you are."

"Your mother already knows I'm a great guy," he

pointed out, starting the truck and backing out of the parking space. "Besides, I thought you promised to keep your nose out of other people's business."

Abby sighed dramatically. "I will, but you two aren't doing anything about this. One dinner date doesn't make you fall in love. Go out lots and lots."

Torn, Zach bit the inside of his cheek.

On the one hand, he agreed with Suzannah that it was important that Abby not interfere with whatever was happening between them. But not a lot *was* happening between them at the moment, so maybe a little interference would help.

He glanced in the rearview mirror and met Abby's gaze. "Tell you what. Call your mom and find out if she wants us to stop on the way and get a pizza for dinner."

A sneaky smile grew on Abby's face. "Yes!"

Zach blew out his breath. Since when was he reduced to using a preteen cupid to help him with his love life? When he was younger, he used to date a lot. In fact, it had just been the last few years that he'd slowed down on the dating. Ever since Keith had died, and he'd started spending most of his free time with Suzannah and Abby.

He'd definitely lost his touch in the dating department, but the more he thought about it, the less he cared. He didn't *want* to still be good at dating a lot of women. He wanted to be good at dating only one woman—Suzannah.

"Yahoo!"

"What is it?"

"Mom says you're an angel for getting pizza and don't forget she likes extra cheese."

He smiled to himself when he realized how much his life had changed. Who would have thought that fast food pizza and a middle school concert sounded like the perfect evening?

There was no doubt about it. He was a changed man.

Suzannah sat between Zach and Edith watching as class after class crossed the stage and sang a few songs. The winter concert had been going on for over almost an hour, and according to the program, two more classes had to sing before Abby's class got its chance.

She wasn't sure how much longer she could take the tension. The evening had felt edgy and wire-drawn.

Ever since Edith had shown up to join them for pizza at the house, Suzannah felt waves of disapproval radiating off her mother-in-law. Nothing Suzannah said seemed to help ease the strain. Even Zach and Abby made several futile attempts to erase the frown that had taken up residence on Edith's face.

"Keith loved attending Abby's little concerts," Edith whispered to Suzannah.

Suzannah sighed. She had tried earlier today to talk to Edith about how much she still loved Keith and how she needed to move on. But her mother-in-law had waved one hand and walked right out of the house.

Leaving Suzannah feeling guilty and frustrated.

When Edith returned for dinner, she acted like nothing had happened.

Suzannah had hoped she could handle things without confrontation, but it was becoming increasingly obvious that she and Edith needed to have a long talk.

Every time Edith mentioned Keith's name, Suzannah felt a pang of remorse. She knew Keith would want her to be happy and to move on, but knowing that and putting it into action were two different things.

Thankfully, Zach seemed to understand what she was going through, and he was being kind and patient with her. She knew he'd like to be alone with her as much as she'd like to be alone with him, but no matter how often they tried, Edith popped up.

"Keith loved watching Abby's concerts," Edith said to Suzannah again, louder this time.

"Yes, I know," Suzannah whispered back. "Zach and I both like them too, and I know you do as well."

Thankfully, before Edith could respond, Abby's class came on stage. As always, Suzannah felt immense pride in her daughter. Abby was a great young lady. She was kind, and smart, and funny. She filled Suzannah's days with such joy and making her daughter happy was Suzannah's main goals. Abby's happiness meant more to her than her own.

At the moment, Abby along with her classmates were singing loudly and enthusiastically. Suzannah felt the joy fill her. She loved this time of the year, and even with all the tension and all the stress, she loved the people here with her tonight. Her daughter was her world, and Zach meant everything to her. She loved him, and even though she didn't know yet if she was *in* love with him, she was half convinced it wouldn't take much for her to be all the way in love.

She also loved Edith. She knew how hard losing Keith had been on her. Losing him still was hard on all of them, but Edith seemed really to be struggling with moving on.

Feeling empathy for her mother-in-law, Suzannah reached over and held her hand.

Edith at first seemed surprised, and then she smiled. The more Suzannah thought about it, the more she realized that Edith needed to know that Suzannah would always love her and be her daughter-in-law, just like Abby would always be her granddaughter.

When Zach started to applaud, Suzannah realized the concert had ended. She stood and gave Edith a hug.

"Let's go get ice cream," Abby announced when she met up with them later. "The Kringle Kafe is having a special for our school. The class that convinces the most people to stop by gets a basket of cool holiday pens and pencils."

Edith declined going with them, saying she wanted to go home and rest. As she started to walk away, she hugged her granddaughter. "You were great tonight."

Abby beamed. "I was, wasn't I?"

Suzannah shot her a "mom" look.

Abby laughed. "What I meant to say was thank you."

Edith laughed. "Yes, that's what I thought you meant to say. You still haven't told me what you want for Christmas. Since Betty wasn't what you wished for, I need to know what is."

Suzannah and Zach both looked at each other. For a second, Suzannah worried that her daughter might tell her grandmother about the Christmas wish she'd shared with her mother and Zach.

Instead, Abby said. "I want a new blow dryer for my hair and lots of hair ties. I'm getting too old to wear it down all the time. Stephie wears her hair in lots of cute styles. I want to do that too."

Edith gave a genuine smile for the first time in a long time. "I'll talk it over with your mother and see what I should get you."

With that, Edith waved and headed off to her car.

Zach looked at Abby. "Since when do you care about your hairstyle?"

Abby giggled. "Since last month. Stephie started

doing her hair differently, and I want to do my hair differently. We're almost grown up."

"Um, no, you're not," Suzannah said. "Ten doesn't mean you're a grownup."

Abby seemed offended. "I'm almost eleven."

Zach nodded slowly. "Which is great. But you have a few more years to go before you're grown up."

"But—"

Gently, he added, "What's great about being almost eleven is that you are old enough to take care of a dog and old enough to be a huge help to your mom. You're very important."

His response seemed to thrill Abby because she grinned and then hugged Zach, and a moment later, her mother.

"I love you guys," she said. "And I forgot to mention, I'm going over to Stephie's house for that ice cream and her folks said we could have a sleep-over if you say yes, but our class still needs *you* to go to the Kringle Kafe so we can win the contest."

Suzannah couldn't believe what her daughter had just done. "You sneak. You planned this all along."

Abby didn't even pretend to be innocent. Instead, she said, "Stephie asked me when I was backstage before the concert, and I thought, why not?"

"You didn't say 'yes' yet, right?" Suzannah asked.

Abby shook her head. "I told her I needed to ask you, but Mom, if I do go with Stephie, then you and Zach can have ice cream alone."

Suzannah glanced at Zach, who seemed as

surprised as she was. Before she said much more to her daughter, Stephie came running over, her mother and stepfather trailing her.

"We're so excited Abby wants to sleep over," said Stephie's mother, Priscilla, a bubbly slender brunette. "She's such a joy to be around."

"She has her moments," Suzannah said and ruffled Abby's hair.

"It is okay with you?"

Abby pressed her palms together.

"All right," Suzannah agreed, not sure she should reward her daughter's underhanded behavior. "But we need to stop by the house first to get her overnight things."

"It's on your way, we can take her," Priscilla offered.

Suzannah shook her head at Abby. "All right," she agreed and leveled a chiding glance at her child. "But your bedtime is still ten. Got it?"

"But tomorrow is Saturday—"

"Ten p.m. or no dice."

"Okay," Abby agreed. Then she and Stephie linked hands and skipped off to her family's vehicle.

"We'll bring her home in the morning," Priscilla promised. "And I'll make sure they are in bed by ten. Although I can't promise I can stop the giggling and talking."

"Thank you," Suzannah said. "It's really nice of you to invite her."

Once Stephie's mom and stepfather followed the girls, Suzannah glanced at Zach.

"She is such a little con artist." She sighed.

"As are a lot of ten-year-olds," he pointed out. "Wheedling to get what they want."

"She twists me around her little finger. If her father were still here, I don't think I'd be so easy to manipulate." Or, if she hadn't wanted so badly to be alone with Zach. Did that make her a terrible mother?

As if reading her mind, Zach placed a reassuring hand on her shoulder. "You're doing a great job with her, Suzie-Q, never doubt it."

"So, do you still want to go to the Kringle Kafe?" She smiled at him.

Zach flashed her another one of his amazing grins. "I would love that."

9

Following the middle school concert, people packed the Kringle Kafe. They were lucky enough to snag a small table by the side window just as two handholding teenagers left.

"Isn't that Dr. Chloe over there?" Zach nodded toward a booth in the far back corner.

"Ooh, she's with a good-looking guy."

"Hey, hey, what about the guy right in front of you?" Zach grinned.

"Don't get jealous." Suzannah laughed. "That guy is *too* pretty. You, my friend, are a ruggedly handsome cowboy. There is absolutely no contest."

He enjoyed hearing her say that. "Who is he?"

Suzannah leaned to the right so she could get a better look. "I don't know, but I'm about to find out."

Before Zach could tell her that it didn't matter, Suzannah headed over to where her boss set with the good-looking stranger.

Zach started to head over to meet the newcomer as well, but he didn't want to risk giving up their table, and a crowd was gathering around Chloe and the stranger.

"What's going on over there?" he asked when Suzannah returned.

"Good grief. So many people want to talk to him," she said. "From what I can gather, his name is Evan Conner. He came here with his boss and Peter Thomas."

"Peter Thomas?" he said it like he had a bad taste in his mouth. People in Kringle disliked Peter Thomas. He'd almost destroyed the small town when he'd bought Kringle Kandy, the largest employer, and moved it to Dallas several years earlier. "Wow. I'd hoped we'd seen the last of that rascal."

Suzannah nodded. "Everyone seems to feel that way, but Peter has had health problems, and he's come home. Apparently, he's had an Ebenezer Scrooge-like transformation."

"Yeah, well in a place called Kringle, that could happen at Christmas," Zach agreed. It was the best time of the year, and people flocked from all over Texas to join in the festivities and bring money into the town.

"But that's no thanks to him," Suzannah muttered.

"How does Chloe know Evan?" Zach asked.

"Peter rented the old Madison house and guess who Evan found inside?"

"Who?"

"Vixen! And she's had puppies."

"That's great. I thought we'd lose her after Vivian Kuhlmeier died. We never could find her." Zach was happy to hear the dog was still alive.

"Chloe is helping take care of Vixen," Suzannah said.

Zach was about to ask more questions when their waitress, Sandy, took their order. They both ordered chocolate pie, deciding it was too cool outside for ice cream.

As Sandy was about to leave, she said, "Strange about Peter Thomas coming back to town. I hope he's not up to something."

"Maybe he really has changed," Suzannah said hopefully. "Everyone deserves the benefit of the doubt."

He liked Suzannah's optimism but personally; he didn't trust the man. "Odd that he would come back to the town where he made so many enemies."

Suzannah nodded slowly. It had impacted her when Kringle Kandy closed. She had worked there, but fortunately when it closed, she could go to work for at Chloe's animal clinic. Not everyone in town had been lucky enough to find work In Kringle.

"Evan said Peter is throwing a big party on Christmas Eve. Everyone's invited."

She held his gaze. "Do you want to go?"

He shook his head. "I don't think so."

"Let's see what happens over the next couple of

weeks. Maybe he's really changed." Suzannah shrugged.

"I'm not sure people ever really do change," Zach said.

"You've changed."

"I have?"

"You used to be a lot more carefree. I remember a young man who used to drag race out on Kringle Flats with his best friend." She canted her head, lowered her lashes and sent him a sidelong glance.

"And who was out there waving the flag to start the race?" he teased.

"I guess we've both changed a bit."

Their pie and coffee arrived. Zach watched as she shook two packets of sugar into her coffee.

"What's so funny?" she asked.

"Nothing."

"Then why are you grinning?"

"I love the way you tear the corner of the sugar packets. Not straight across like most people, but that cute little half circle fold."

"You're easily amused, buster." She laughed again, and it was a beautiful sound that warmed him from the center of his solar plexus out to his fingers and toes.

"So what's this I hear about decorating a float?" he asked, watching her slowly stir the sugar in her coffee. "I thought Mayor Holton conned us into riding on the town hall float as Santa and Mrs. Claus."

"We *are* riding on the town hall float," she said. "But Abby's class needs help with their float. Do you have any time to help?"

If he were honest, he'd say no. Looking at her now across the table, he admitted to her, "I'll do anything you want me to."

At first she laughed a little nervously, as if he was kidding, but then she straightened and blinked and said, "Do you really mean that?"

"You know you have me wrapped around your little finger," he confessed. "You and Abby both."

"Zach," she said in such an odd tone that he felt a small kick of fear in the pit of his stomach.

Had he confessed too much?

"Yes?"

"You have no idea how much I appreciate you."

"I—"

Someone put some raucous tune on the jukebox and he couldn't talk to her without shouting over the noise. Perhaps it was for the best. This crowded diner wasn't the place to have a serious conversation.

It could wait until they got to her house.

Since Abby was spending the night at Stephie's they would be all alone. That thought quickened his pulse.

But as they were leaving the cafe, Suzannah got a text from her daughter. Worry pursed her lips.

"Something wrong?" Zach asked.

"Abby's cut her leg. Stephie's folks have bandaged it, but we need to swing by and pick her up."

"Is she okay?" he asked, holding the door open for Suzannah. Outside, they headed to his truck.

"She's fine. She's just out of the sleepover spirit now and wants to come home," Suzannah said, sounding just a little worried once they buckled in the cab. "And I have to admit I want her home. I can't relax until I see her in person and know she's okay."

"Me too." He reached across the seat to squeeze her hand. "We're on the way to her now."

"So much for our evening alone." She gave him a wry smile.

"I've waited this long for you, Suzannah," he said. "No harm in waiting a little longer."

I've waited this long for you, Suzannah. Zach's words circled Suzannah's head as they drove to pick up her daughter.

The cab of his truck seemed weighted with meaning and expectation. Neither of them spoke during the short trip to Stephie's house, but Suzannah was hyperaware of him. His strong hands on the steering wheel, the tangy scent of his masculine cologne, his deep-throated sound as he hummed along with the Christmas tune on the radio.

Her body grew warm and tingled, her attraction to him growing stronger with each passing moment.

It was confusing, this new and surprising chemistry with her best friend.

The man who had once been her late husband's best friend.

She pushed the thoughts from her mind. This wasn't the time or place. They retrieved Abby and took her home.

"What happened exactly," Suzannah asked as Abby climbed into the truck.

"It was the coolest thing. Stephie and I were dancing to a Billie Eilish YouTube video, and I tripped over the little purple rug in her room and crashed into her dresser. Stephie grabbed the mirror right before it fell, so at least I didn't break that."

"Then how did you cut yourself?" Suzannah asked.

"On her music box. I broke it but I'll buy her a new one from my piggy bank allowance."

"That's responsible of you, but you should be more careful, Abby."

"It's only a bitty cut, Mom," she said. "But don't tell the kids at school. Stephie and I decided we'll tell them it's a big gash."

"No, you won't," Suzannah said. "That would be lying. Plus, you're lucky it *isn't* a big gash. You could have needed stitches."

"I know," Abby said.

Once they were inside the house, Abby went upstairs to count the money in her piggy bank.

Suzannah followed her and sank down on her

daughter's bed. She didn't say the words that hovered on her lips, but she felt them like a gut punch. She couldn't bear it if something terrible happened to Abby. Keith's death had almost destroyed her, and Abby was her entire world.

When her daughter had called tonight to say she'd gotten hurt, for a moment, Suzannah had felt like someone grabbed her heart and squeezed. The fear had been overwhelming, and even now, she still felt shaken and upset. She didn't want to be a helicopter mom, but sometimes she really struggled to control her fears.

Movement in the hall captured her attention, and she glanced up.

Zach was standing in the doorway, his hands tucked into the front pockets of his jeans. He met her gaze and gave her a soft smile. Having him here tonight had helped a lot. She always felt calmer when Zach was around.

"Since she's okay, I guess I'll head home," he said.

"Mom, why don't you walk him to his truck? Men aren't the only ones who should have manners." A devious grin hopped onto her daughter's face.

"You are so transparent, kiddo, but I will walk him to the front door so I can lock it behind him." Suzannah got up.

"Hey Zach," Abby said. "Do you have any chores I can do on your ranch to earn money? I only have four dollars. I've got to replace Stephie's music box."

Zach met Suzannah's gaze and arched an eyebrow.

She nodded.

Zach shrugged. "Sure, I have chores you can do. We always need someone to muck out the horse stalls."

Abby crinkled her nose. "Umm, okay, I guess."

Chuckling, Zach shook his head and Suzannah joined him.

"You don't have to pay her for chores," she said as they walked downstairs together. "Just let her do a few things so she understands the importance of paying for her mistakes."

"I'm happy to pay her, Suzannah. I wasn't kidding when I said there are lots of chores on a ranch."

Although she knew he didn't mean it that way, Suzannah suddenly realized how selfish she had been, especially recently, relying on Zach too much. Expecting him to show up for her when he had so much work of his own.

"I am so sorry," she said as they reached the front door. "I just realized that Abby and I pull you away from your ranch too often. You have things you need to do. We've been inconsiderate."

She wasn't sure what reaction she expected, but it wasn't the one she got.

He spun on his heels to face her. "Suzannah, I love every minute I spend with you and Abby, and I only wish I could spend even more time with the two of you."

"Oh," she said, surprised by the fierce tenderness on his face.

He wrapped his arms around her in a loose hug. "In case you haven't noticed, I'm really fond of the two of you."

She expected him to kiss her, but when he didn't, she realized he was waiting to see what she would do. So she did what she'd been wanting to do all evening, she leaned in and kissed him.

Unlike the kiss in his truck, this kiss was long and slow. Zach gathered her close and kissed her so hard she felt it all the way to her toes.

Then suddenly, it was over.

He abruptly broke off the kiss and met her confused gaze. "We are being watched."

Suzannah signed and moved out of his embrace. Turning, she saw her daughter standing at the top of the stairs with Betty in her arms and an expression of pure delight on her face.

Winking, Zach said "goodnight" to them both and left.

Suzannah locked the door behind him. "Don't say a word," she said, walking past her daughter and heading toward her bedroom. "And don't read too much into that kiss. It was just a friendly kiss. We aren't in love, and we aren't getting married. Now be a nice young lady and go to bed."

"Sure, Mom." Abby giggled. "Whatever you say."

10

"There's so much yucky stuff in this barn." It was Saturday morning and Abby was helping Zach muck out the stables. "Why are all the chores on a ranch gross and stinky?"

"Because animals make messes," he said. "And unlike Betty, my horses aren't house trained, or in this case, stall trained."

Abby turned and looked at him. "Why not? Why can't horses get stall trained?"

Zach started to tell her they just couldn't, but then he considered her question. "You know, I think they can. At least, somewhat. I must look into that. I don't think it will be quite the same as Betty, but maybe there could be some progress."

Abby beamed. "See? I know stuff. Maybe one day I'll have a horse, and I can try housebreaking it."

"Or at least barn broken." He chuckled, enjoying her company. "You're a smart kid, that's for sure."

"I get it from my mom," she said.

Zach had been in the middle of loading another pitchfork full of soiled straw into the wheelbarrow and he stopped. "And your dad."

Abby glanced at him. "What?"

"You get your intelligence from your mom *and* your dad. Your mom's a smart lady, but your dad was very smart, too."

"Was he?"

Zach went back to clearing the soiled straw. "Yeah. He was one of the smartest people I've ever met. He was so smart, he didn't have to try too hard in school and always got straight As. He learned quick."

Abby bobbed her head. "I'm like that. My teachers all say I learn stuff very quickly but I don't apply myself." She giggled at that last part.

Zach smiled at her. She looked so much like her mother that sometimes he only saw that, but when she talked, she sounded a lot like her dad. "Like I said, you're a bright kid."

They worked for a while in silence, then Abby said, "I think Dad would like it if you married my mom."

Zach had been expecting her to say something all morning. After she'd seen him kissing Suzannah, he wasn't surprised that she assumed those things.

"You know, your mom and I are great friends, and maybe something will happen someday..."

"I knew it," Abby half screamed, jumped up and down.

"Whoa...whoa," he said. "Let me finish."

It took a few moments for her to settle. When she finally calmed, Zach said, "But maybe nothing will happen between us, Abby. Let us figure things out on our own. You can't rush this."

Abby acted like a balloon with the air let out. She spent the next half hour moping and muttering.

Finally, Zach said, "Don't do that. If you want to act grown up, learn to accept things the way they are. You can't force people to do what you want. Let your mother and me determine what's best for us."

He wasn't sure how he expected her to react, and he was glad when she surprised him by nodding. "You're right. I know I told you this is my Christmas wish, and it is, but you and Mom have to decide if it is *your* Christmas wish as well."

"Thank you."

"I promise to not push on you. I just thought when I saw you kissing that maybe—"

"I know," he said, understanding her confusion. "But you have to let us figure this out on our own."

Abby sighed loudly. "Fine. I'll stay out of it. But just so you know, I'm not changing my Christmas wish, and if Kringle is half as magical around Christmas as everyone says, my wish will come true."

She might have sounded grown up there for a moment, but she was still a kid at heart. And Zach also hoped her Christmas wish would come true.

Suzannah looked at the slow cooker sitting on the seat next to her, along with a pan of fresh hot cornbread. She knew her homemade chili was Zach's favorite, and she'd cooked it with him in mind.

She wanted to thank him for letting Abby work on his ranch, and also for helping decorate for the concert, and just so many things he'd done for them not just recently, but over the last few years.

Even tonight, he was helping to decorate the float for Abby. She wanted to let him know that he didn't need to help. He'd already done so much.

As shameful as it seemed, until recently, she hadn't stopped to consider how selfish she and Abby were being so frequently asking for his help. She just assumed he wanted to be around because he'd always been so close to Keith and he never complained.

But now that she was seeing things from his point of view, she felt terrible. Not only had he probably needed more time to spend working on his ranch, but he also might have wanted time to date. Had she prevented him from finding someone sooner, someone to fall in love with?

She had mixed feelings about that thought, but she knew that was selfish as well. She had leaned hard on him over the years, and now she was here to offer chili and an apology.

When she got to the ranch, she parked in front of his red brick ranch-style house. She knew he'd be in the barn at this time of day, so she brought the food inside the kitchen and set it on the counter. Then, she headed toward the barn.

She found him inside working. At the moment, he was standing by one of his horse stalls, talking to Caleb Sutton, a neighboring rancher.

"Hey, what brings you here?" Zach asked. He walked over and without a word, kissed her lightly. "It's so good to see you."

Suzannah was both surprised and thrilled by his kiss, and in front of Caleb, as if he wasn't the least bit embarrassed to have everyone know they were dating.

"It's good to see you, too," she said, slipping her arm around his waist as they turned toward Caleb. Like Zach, Caleb was tall with dark hair, but unlike Zach's deep brown eyes, Caleb had light gray eyes.

"So, I was going to ask what's new with you, Suzannah, but I guess I can see for myself." Caleb grinned.

"Yes, a few things have changed. And hey, Abby and I were on your ranch recently. We swung by Kringle Kritter Rescue and she adopted a dog," Zach said.

"That's great," Caleb said. "The Millers run a terrific shelter. I'm always glad to hear when a dog gets adopted."

"Betty is a sweetheart," Suzannah said. "It's so nice that you donated the land to the Millers to run their rescue."

"I love animals." He shrugged. "Just like Zach. And the Millers are a great couple. They've done a lot to rescue and then find homes for hundreds of stray and abandoned animals."

"It's a great rescue. Now that Ava's back, maybe she can help her folks run it," Suzannah said.

At the mention of Ava Miller's name, Caleb frowned, but said nothing. Did he not like Ava?

Caleb shook Zach's hand. "See you in a little while." With a smile at Suzannah, he added, "And I'll see both at the parade, and I also hope to see you at Home for the Holidays."

Suzannah had almost forgotten that the rescue organization was holding a special adoption event on the day after the parade. It thrilled her the event was getting a big buzz. Hopefully, lots of dogs and cats will get adopted.

After Caleb left, Suzannah turned to Zach. "Looks like I shouldn't have mentioned Ava."

Zach shrugged. "There's a lot of history between Caleb and Ava. Time will tell how that works out."

Suzannah hadn't meant to step on a sore spot. "I'll avoid mentioning her. But why was Caleb here? And why is he coming back later?"

"I'm buying another horse," Zach said. "Caleb has the best horses around. He'll be back in a few minutes."

Curious, Suzannah asked, "Why are you buying another horse?"

A broad grin crossed Zach's face. "I thought Abby

might want a horse to ride now that she's older. She always is so interested when she's here, and I'd love to teach her to ride if it's okay with—"

"Oh, my!"

Suzannah couldn't believe how thoughtful he was. Abby had always wanted to learn to ride. It amazed that he had bought her a horse.

At a loss for how to thank him, Suzannah wrapped her arms around his neck and kissed him.

"Wow," he said and rubbed his mouth. "I should buy horses for your daughter more often."

"You are so thoughtful."

"Thank you, ma'am. Can I surprise her for Christmas?"

Suzannah nodded, and for a second, she almost said that it would be a nice surprise along with getting her Christmas wish, but she still wasn't bold enough to say that. She was confident enough. Even if she and Zach continued along the path they were on, they might not be ready to decide they were officially a couple by Christmas.

"I think she'll love Pearl," he said.

"Pearl?"

"It's the horse I'm buying for her. She's Caleb's gentlest horse, and a real sweetheart."

"That's so sweet of you," she said and kissed him again.

"I could really get used to this." He grinned. "So why are you here? I thought we were meeting in town later to decorate the parade float."

"We are, but I thought I'd stop by with some chili and cornbread. Thank you for everything you do for us. I know Abby and I lean on you constantly, and I'm so sorry that I didn't realize until recently just how much. It's been unfair to you."

He seemed surprised. "I appreciate the thought, but I enjoy every second I spend with you. I love you both."

His words caught her off guard, and she wanted to ask him exactly what type of love he meant, but before she could, Caleb returned with the horse.

"Hope I'm not interrupting anything," he said, walking in leading a beautiful black mare. "Suzannah, meet Pearl. So named because she's as beautiful as a black pearl."

Suzannah walked over and patted the horse. "I hope she's as gentle as she seems. Abby's a beginner."

"She's the sweetest thing in the world," Caleb said. "And Zach will teach Abby the right way to ride and care for her."

Suzannah watched them get Pearl settled in the barn. As much as she wanted to stay, she had to pick up Abby so they could go decorate the float.

"Why don't you stay with Pearl and forget decorating the float," she said.

Zach started to protest, but she held up one hand. "You have done so much for us and getting this horse for Abby is a wonderful surprise. You're an amazing man, Zach Delaney."

"You're pretty amazing yourself," he said, giving her a quick kiss. "Thanks for dinner."

She laughed, happy beyond belief. As she headed back to her car, she couldn't help thinking that maybe she wouldn't need as much time as she'd thought to adjust to this new relationship with Zach.

Every day, she fell a little more in love with him.

"Thanks again for selling me Pearl," Zach said. "I know you planned to hold on to her."

"I did because I wanted her to have a special home, which she now has." Caleb motioned toward the slow cooker full of chili and when Zach nodded, he helped himself to more of the chili Suzannah had brought. "Man, this chili's great."

Zach laughed. "Yeah, it's terrific. Suzannah is a good cook."

"Seems like you two have changed your relationship recently," he said. "I thought you two were just friends."

"We were," he said. "Then Abby told us her Christmas wish was for her mom and me to fall in love and get married. Guess it got both of us thinking that maybe our relationship should head in a new direction."

Caleb nodded, then said, "How's Edith doing with that?"

"I don't think she likes it. I know this is very hard for her. Hard for all of us."

"Keith was a great guy," Caleb said. "But he'd want everyone to be happy."

Zach nodded. "Yeah, I know he would, and I think Suzannah feels that as well. For Edith, though, it will be hard because he was her only child. I think she's worried we'll forget Keith."

"Then make sure you don't," Caleb said. "Seems like what the two of you have together is worth fighting for. Maybe you should find a way so that everyone is happy."

Zach nodded slowly, turning Caleb's words over in his mind. Maybe that was what he needed to do. Make sure that they remember Keith.

But how?

Keith had been a great guy, and he'd deserved better than to die so young. But since he couldn't do anything about that, maybe he could do something else to help keep his memory alive.

That got Zach's mental cogs whirling.

11

"Mom, that man keeps putting the black dots on wrong," Abby said, coming over to stand next to her mother. She was speaking about Evan Connor, who Dr. Chloe had recruited to help them decorate the float.

"Abby," she murmured. "Don't be rude."

"We need more black paper," Abby said. "I'll go get it."

Before Suzannah could say anything, Abby darted across the parking lot to where the supplies were stashed in the back of Chloe's vet van.

What was Abby talking about? Confused, she walked over to the side of the float where Evan Conner was working. She looked at the black dots he'd glued onto the white butcher's paper they had wrapped around the flatbed trailer. The dots looked fine to her.

"Your daughter told me I'm doing this all wrong."

He straightened and scratched his head. "But the dots look aligned to me."

"I think she means they might look better scattered around. She's got an artistic eye, and she's brutally honest," Suzannah said. "I've been trying to teach her how to be tactfully truthful, but it doesn't seem to work. She's nailed the truthful part. Not so much the tactful part."

"She is right, though. I'm bad at this," Evan muttered.

"Let's see if we can move a few."

Thankfully, since the glue was still damp, they could shift two of the spots so they were no longer in a row.

"That looks better," Evan said.

After a few moments, Chloe and Abby returned with more black paper. When they reached the truck, Abby said to Evan, "You're frowning like Scrooge."

"Bah Humbug to you too," Evan said, then glanced at Chloe. "Did she tell you that I'm doing a bad job?"

"Abby reported your failings," Chloe said, sounding stern but undoing the effect by grinning. "I know you warned me that you are bad at this sort of thing, but I had no idea how true that was. Thank goodness Abby was here to save the day."

Abby beamed at Chloe's praise and she pointed at the offending spots. "I'm going to help him. I'm good at decorating."

Evan smiled at Abby. "Is that so?"

Abby bobbed her head. "Yes, I've been helping Dr. Anderson since I was little. She says I'm the best worker she has. When I grow up, I'm going to be a vet just like her."

Suzannah walked over to her daughter. "That's all Abby's ever wanted to be, so I guess I'd better save for college now."

"Yes. You'll want to get a definite head start," Evan said. "Vet school isn't cheap."

"True." Suzannah had already put away a little money for Abby's college tuition, and she got Keith's death benefits, but she needed to save even more to make sure Abby could attend whatever school she wanted.

Just thinking about it, though, made her nervous. It was a lot of money to save in the next few years.

Her frown must have given away because Evan said, "I'll give you some investment tips to grow your savings if you'd like."

"You would do that for me?"

"Any friend of Chloe's is a friend of mine." Evan smiled.

"Thank you so much," Suzannah said.

"In the meantime," Abby announced. "We've got a float to decorate." She grinned and sat on the cement floor and started cutting out black dots of various sizes.

Seeing that her daughter was happily working again, Suzannah returned to the front of the vehicle.

"So who's riding in this float?" Evan asked.

"Santa and Mrs. Claus!" She leaned forward and loudly whispered to Evan. "Mrs. Claus is my mom this year, and Santa is Zach Delaney."

Evan glanced at Suzannah. "Mrs. Claus? Really? Well, you have held up well over the years."

Chloe laughed. "Suzannah and Zach are good sports to jump in at the last moment. Usually the Millers, an older couple who live just outside of town do it, but this year, they can't make it."

"Zach and I are happy to help," Suzannah said.

Over the next couple of hours, they worked on the Christmas float. On the way home, Abby chattered about her plans of being a vet.

Although Suzannah was listening, part of her mind was worrying about paying for college and then vet school. Abby was serious about this, she was going to need a lot of money, and there was no guarantee that she would get scholarships and she hated for Abby to have to take on astronomical school loans.

Which meant if she and Zach got married, would he feel responsible for helping put Abby through school? She knew he loved her daughter, but it didn't seem fair to ask him to take on that kind of commitment.

She needed to slow things down. There was so much more to think about having a relationship with Zach than whether they would make a compatible as a couple.

Zach was the kind of man who would say it didn't matter, but it *did*. Abby's college bills would be as high as a hundred thousand dollars or more. She couldn't ask him to take on a wife with that kind of obligation.

Sadness engulfed Suzannah like a net. She was going to have to think about this seriously. If she married Zach, she became his wife and Abby became his daughter. He might not be legally responsible for Abby, but she knew he was the kind of man who would insist on paying. He might even want to adopt Abby, but Suzannah didn't see that as possible. Abby needed to stay Abby Owens and know that her father had loved her deeply.

Suzannah was still thinking about it when they got home to find Edith was sitting in the living room, petting Betty.

Stunned, Suzannah stared at her. Her mother-in-law's car hadn't been in the driveway, which must mean Edith had walked the four blocks over to their house.

"Well, there you two are!" Edith said. "I didn't realize you wouldn't be home this evening."

"Grandma," Abby said. "I'm glad you were careful when you came in. I haven't gotten Betty trained yet. She might try to run off."

Edith handed the dog to Abby. "I was careful, but I would not stand outside in the cold waiting for you to get home. I'm still part of this family. Your father may no longer be here, but I am."

Suzannah didn't miss the sternness in Edith's stern, and she almost said something, but she stopped herself. She wasn't about to scold her mother-in-law with her daughter in the room, but she needed to have a long talk with Edith.

She sent Abby off to play with Betty, and then she sat down across from her mother-in-law. "Edith, you mean the world to Abby and me, but please don't come into my house when I'm not home."

Edith frowned. "So now I'm not welcome in my son's house?"

Suzannah had feared Edith would take it this way, but she had to make her boundaries clear. Taking care to keep her voice gentle, she said, "That's not true at all. You are *always* welcome, and you always will be. But Abby and I don't simply walk into your house when you're not home. We always knock and wait for you to invite us in. We will always invite you into the house, but we have a right to our privacy."

"This is so you can date Zach, right? You don't want me stopping by because you want to have that man over here all the time." Edith's frown deepened.

Suzannah took a deep breath. She could see the pain on Edith's face. She crossed the room and sat next to her. "You mean the world to me, Edith. You also mean the world to Abby. We love you, and we will always love you. But Keith wouldn't want me to be alone for the rest of my life. You raised a wonderful man, and I miss him desperately every day. But Abby and I need to build a new life for ourselves, and yes, that life may involve me falling in love again."

"With Zach?"

Tears had formed in Edith's eyes, and Suzannah felt her own eyes whelm up. "I don't know. Asking Zach to take on the burden of a family is unfair. He's a great guy, such a great guy that he would feel obligated to give up everything that means something to him to make us happy. Abby wants to become a vet, and I've realized it is unfair to ask another person to take on the financial burden."

Her explanation seemed to startle Edith. "I don't dislike Zach, and he seems like a man who wouldn't mind. I do know he really loves Abby. He'd want to see her succeed."

Suzannah nodded. "Yes, I know. But because he's such a great guy, he would give up everything for Abby. I can't ask him to do that."

"But he'd want to," Edith said. "It's hard for me to see you with someone other than my son, but I will say that Zach seems like a good man. I know Keith thought he was a good guy."

Suzannah couldn't help smiling. Suddenly rather than lambasting Zach, Edith was defending him. But it didn't matter. Suzannah had decided.

"He is a good guy, and that's why I've decided we will just stay friends. I couldn't ask him to take on this responsibility because I know he wouldn't think twice about accepting it. I know he would gladly give up everything for Abby, and I can't let him do it."

Edith grabbed a tissue and dabbed at her eyes. "You know, Keith would hate that you feel this way. You're pushing away love."

Suzannah knew she was, and but it was because she loved Zach that she'd decided she needed to return to just being Zach's friend.

It was the right thing to do for the man she loved.

Zach felt like a lurker sitting in his truck in front of Edith's house waiting for her to come home. A brighter man might wait until tomorrow to talk to her, but he was feeling pressure to put this topic to rest.

He was about to give up and head home when Edith walked up. She saw him and waved. Even though it was getting dark, he could clearly see her expression.

She seemed excited to see him.

"I'm glad you're here. I was going to call you tonight. You need to come inside so we can talk," she said, hurrying up the path to her house and quickly unlocking the front door.

Of all the receptions he'd expected, this possibility had never crossed his mind. Edith seemed happy to see him.

Once they got inside, he cleared his throat, preparing to launch into all the reasons he wanted Edith to understand that his love for Suzannah in no way took away from what she'd shared with Keith, but he never got that far.

"Keith wants to pay for Abby's college expenses. You can't do it," Edith said.

Zach didn't mean to be impolite, but what in the blazes was she talking about. "I'm a little confused, Edith. I came here because I wanted to talk to you about Suzannah. I'm in love with her, and I know this is difficult for you to accept, but just because we're in love doesn't mean we still don't love and miss Keith."

Edith patted his arm. "I know. I realize that now."

Relief flooded through Zach. The last thing he wanted to do was to cause Edith more pain. She'd been through so much these last few years.

"I'm glad," he said. "Keith was a wonderful man who would want Suzannah to be happy."

Edith nodded, then said, "But she won't be happy. She'll call things off with you."

That couldn't be true. When she left the ranch this afternoon, everything had been fine. In fact, it had been more than fine. Everything had been great.

"Why would she do that? I'm sorry if this upsets you, Edith, I truly am, but—"

Edith waved her hands and cut him off. "It's not because of me. I realize that Keith would want her to be happy. It's just hard."

Zach nodded. "I know."

"But that isn't the problem," she said. "She will break things off so that you don't pay for Abby's college tuition."

Zach had to admit, he might not be the brightest star in the sky, but he hadn't a clue what she was talking about. "Abby's ten," he said. "She won't go to college for eight years."

"I know, I know. But when she does, it will cost a fortune if she doesn't get scholarships," Edith said. "Stay here. I'll be right back."

Edith scurried out the room, leaving Zach standing in the middle of her living room feeling confused. He glanced around. Everywhere he looked there were pictures of Keith's smiling face. Those pictures made his heart ache for Edith.

When she came back into the room, she was carrying a piece of paper. "When Keith was born, I started buying five-hundred dollar savings bonds twice a year, on his birthday and on Christmas. I kept buying them figuring I'd use them for his college, but he got a scholarship. Then I kept buying them thinking I'd give them to him on his last birthday..." She trailed off.

Zach understood why. Keith had died far too young.

Edith took a deep breath and continued, "I still kept buying them since he died. I wasn't sure what I would do with them until today. Keith will pay for Abby's college education. Not you. Not Suzannah. Keith. This will be from him to his daughter, and I don't want anyone to argue with me."

Zach wanted to point out that he would be happy to pay for Abby's college education, but he understood why it meant so much to Edith. This was something Keith could do for his daughter.

"I think that's a great idea, but have you talked to Suzannah?"

Edith shook her head. "Not yet. I wanted to talk to you first. Are you in love with Suzannah? Do you plan to marry her?"

Zach felt strange having this conversation with Edith before he'd even had it with Suzannah, but he figured getting Edith on his side was a little like getting Keith's nod of approval.

"Yes, I'm in love with Suzannah. I've been in love with her for a long, long time. And yes, I want to marry her," he said.

A huge smile crossed Edith's face, and he realized it had been years since he had seen her happy. "That's great. Then you need to tell her before she tells you she wants to call it off. Also tell her about Keith's gift to Abby. She's his daughter, and it's only right."

Zach agreed that he needed to talk to Suzannah soon, but first he needed to do something else. A phone call to Dave Holton should take care of it.

Before he headed out to his truck, though, he needed to say something to Keith's mother.

"Thank you, Edith, for everything. I promise to love Suzannah and Abby with all my heart."

She took a step forward and hugged him. "I know you will."

12

Suzannah felt like she was going to explode. As she was getting dressed in her Mrs. Claus costume, all she could think about was the difficult conversation she needed to have with Zach.

She was going to have to tell him that they could only be friends. As much as the thought broke her heart, she knew it was the right thing to do. Chloe had received scholarships to help with some of her tuition, but she still had student loans which she was paying, and it was years since she had gotten out of college.

Suzannah couldn't stand the thought of Abby struggling with that debt. She would take on the debt for her daughter, and she would be happy to do it. But it was unfair and wrong to have Zach take on the burden, even if he wanted to.

She was pacing by the float on which she was Zach would ride when she finally saw him across the parking lot. She twisted her hands as he approached. He looked handsome even in his Santa costume.

"Hi," he said when he reached her. "You look beautiful."

She smiled, but she knew her smile was weak. She hated what she had to do, but it was the only fair thing. She realized the kind move would be to wait until after the parade was over to tell him, but she just couldn't. Instead, she blurted, "We need to just be friends. I'm sorry."

Rather than looking crestfallen, Zach nodded slowly. "Edith told me you would say that."

Suzannah felt tears forming in her eyes. "I'm sorry. This isn't about Keith. It's about—" She waved one hand, knowing if she tried to explain he would argue with her. "It's lots of things. Let's just be friends, ok?"

Zach started to say something, but the mayor, Dave Holton, walked over.

"It's time for the happy couple to take their places." He helped Suzannah climb onto the truck. Then he turned to Zach. "It's all set."

Suzannah had no clue what Dave meant. She waited until Zach jumped up on the truck and sat in his chair next to hers. "What's all set?"

Rather than answering her question, he smiled at her. "Everything will be okay."

Suzannah sighed. Zach didn't understand, and she didn't have time right now to explain. She slowly shook her head. "No. It's not. We need to talk."

He leaned over and gave her a slow, soft kiss, and despite her best intentions, she kissed him back.

"We will talk as soon as the parade is over," he said. "But don't worry. Things will work out."

"Hey, Mr. and Mrs. Claus, stop necking. We need to start this parade," Dave said, climbing into the driver's seat of the truck. "Let's go wow the people of Kringle."

Before Suzannah could say more, the parade started. She felt terrible about how things turned out with Zach, and she realized she should have waited until after the parade to tell him. But waiting to tear off a bandage didn't make it hurt less.

Sometimes you need to just go through the pain. You had to, if you wanted to reach the other side.

Zach couldn't remember the last time he'd felt this encouraged. He knew deep in his heart that things with Suzannah would work out, and he'd never been happier.

He glanced at her. She was so sad, and he wanted to tell her about his discussion with Edith, but he felt strongly that Edith needed to tell her the news. It was important that Keith be part of this decision.

As the parade slowly wove its way through town, Zach kept up a steady stream of "ho ho ho" and tossed candy to the children. The crowd was huge this year. It seemed like every year, Kringle drew more and more people to their festivities. He couldn't blame them. Kringle was a great town, but around Christmas, it took on an almost magical feel. Abby was right. Christmas in Kringle made you believe in wishes.

And speaking of Abby, she was on the float in front of them. She and Chloe dressed as elves and looked really cute. They'd left Betty at the clinic so that the parade didn't over excite her. Several times, she grinned and waved at her mom and Zach. He waved back. She didn't know it yet, but hopefully, she was about to get her wish.

The parade took almost an hour to weave through the city. Several times they stopped and little ones came over and sat on his lap. He was getting better at handling the children and making sure they believed in him. He knew that his role was about more than simply pretending to be Santa. It was about teaching children to dream and believe.

Once they reached the end of the parade route, everyone climbed off the floats and gathered in the staging area. Zach scanned the crowd until he spotted Edith. They agreed that she would meet them at the end of the parade. She was smiling and waving enthusiastically.

He was thrilled to see she felt much better about everything, and he completely understood why it was important to have Keith be part of this along with her. As much as he wanted to assure her that he would make sure Abby had everything she needed in life, he knew this was one time when he needed to put his ego aside and do what was best for Abby and Edith.

He turned and helped Suzannah off the float. He could tell she was trying not to cry, and he felt terrible that he couldn't make her feel better immediately, but he needed to let Edith explain this first.

"Zach, we need to talk," Suzannah said once they were both standing on the ground.

"I know," he told her. "And we will. But first, we need to go see Edith." He took her hand and led her over to where Abby was standing. When she saw them, Abby hugged both her mom and Zach.

"Wasn't that fun? All the kids seemed really excited." Abby was bouncing up and down. "Lots of them waved to me too."

Suzannah hugged her daughter again. "They did. Who doesn't love a cute elf?"

Abby giggled, then noticed her grandmother standing across the parking lot. "Look. Grandma is here," she said before sprinting toward the older woman.

Zach turned to head that way, but Suzannah grabbed his hand. "Wait. I need to talk to you before we see Edith. I've given us lots of thought, and I really don't think we should try to be more than friends. I'm sorry, Zach. I know this is hard, but it's for the best. Things are just not going to work out for us."

Zach knew it upset her, so he leaned down and

lightly kissed her on the cheek. "You need to have faith," he said. "Believe in the Christmas magic of Kringle, just like Abby."

Before Suzannah could say anything else, he took her hand and together they headed across the parking lot to talk to Edith.

~

Things were not going well, Suzannah decided as she walked with Zach across the parking lot. She needed to talk to him and get this over with before she started to sob. Breaking up with him was the right thing to do, she knew it deep within her heart, but going through it was hard. The sooner she could get it over, the better.

But life was not on her side. Every few feet, someone stopped them to talk about the parade, comment on their costumes, or take a picture with them. Knowing that the last thing people wanted to see was a sad Mrs. Claus, she forced herself to put on a happy face. Just because her heart was breaking didn't mean she had the right to ruin this occasion for others.

"Santa and Mrs. Claus, I'd like to introduce you to my grandson, Tyson," Dave Holton said, holding the hand of his young grandson. Although Suzannah had met Tyson several times over the years, she realized that Mrs. Claus never had.

"It's nice to meet you," she said to the young man

who was smiling up at her with a big grin. Before she could say anything else, he hugged her leg.

"I luff you," he said, his eyes shining. "I luff you lots." Then he tipped his head and looked up at Zach, his eyes wide. "Wow."

Zach crouched down so he was level with Tyson. "Ho, ho, ho," he said. "It's nice to meet you."

"I've been good," Tyson said, rubbing Zach's beard with fingers that appeared more than a little sticky. "I luff you a lot."

Tyson was melting her heart. Suzannah loved children and watching Zach as he talked and laughed with Tyson caused her to decide she was making things even harder. She and Keith had always planned to have more children, but it wasn't to be. Now, knowing that she needed to focus on Abby and her future, that was a dream she should probably let go of. She had Abby, and she was happy.

Well, at least she would be once she got over losing her relationship with Zach.

After Tyson gave them both more hugs, they walked over to join Edith.

"Dave's grandson is really cute," Edith said, looking at Suzannah. "Children are such a gift."

Suzannah nodded. She was finding it increasingly difficult to remain calm. "Yes, Abby and her future mean everything to me."

Before she could add more, Edith hugged Abby and then told Suzannah, "She means everything to me too. And to Keith. Which is why he wants to do something for his daughter."

Suzannah blinked. She wasn't sure where Edith was going with this. "I'm sorry, but I don't understand."

Edith came to stand directly in front of Suzannah. Then she said, "I have been buying savings bonds since the day Keith was born. Every birthday and Christmas, I bought them. I was saving them for his college tuition, but he didn't need them because they awarded him scholarships. Then I saved them for his thirtieth birthday, but sadly we lost him before then."

Suzannah felt her throat closing up. Thinking about losing Keith was hard at the best of times. Today, when she was already feeling so emotional, she was having trouble not crying.

"I'm so sorry," she said to Edith. "Keith would have been so surprised by your gift."

Edith patted her arm. "I know, dear. I like to think of the bonds as belonging to him, which is why I know he would want to give them to Abby to use for college."

Suzannah started to say something, then she stopped and admitted, "Edith, I don't understand."

Edith smiled and hugged Abby. "Keith would want his daughter to have the money to pursue her dreams."

"But it's your money," Suzannah pointed out. "You should keep it for yourself."

Edith shook her head. "No. That wouldn't make

me happy. What will make me happy is knowing that this is something Keith can do for his daughter."

When Suzannah started to protest, Edith said, "Please, dear. This is very important to me. It is something Keith can do."

Suzannah didn't know what to say, but she understood why this meant so much to Edith. "That's so sweet."

Abby hugged her grandmother. "That's so cool, Grandma. Thank you so much. I love you, and I love Daddy."

Edith's smile was just a little wobbly as she said, "I know, sweetheart. We all do."

After Abby finished hugging her grandmother, Suzannah hugged her. "You're so kind."

Edith laughed softly. "It makes me thrilled to do this for Abby. It also means that you no longer have an excuse for not being happy yourself."

Edith's words surprised her. She hadn't been thinking about her situation, but now that Edith pointed it out, she was right. Zach would no longer feel responsible.

She looked at him. He was smiling at Edith. "She's a very special lady, isn't she?"

"I can't believe she is doing this," Suzannah said. "I was so worried about Abby's future, and I didn't want—"

"Me to feel obligated to pay for it, right?" He gathered her close and said, "You know, if we're going to make this marriage work, know I'm all in. This is a partnership. You and Abby will be my family. Everything I have is yours."

"Everything I have is yours, too," she told him, loving flowing through her. "I love you so much."

He grinned. "Good, because I have one more surprise for everyone." He walked over to where Dave stood. "I want to thank the mayor for helping me pull together a last-minute surprise."

With a great deal of flourish, Dave pulled a cord and open a banner on the side of the empty store building that abutted the parking lot. The banner read Keith J. Owens Community Center.

"I want to thank Za—I mean Santa Claus for buying the building and donating it to the city. I know Keith would be proud. The city can really use this center. We have great plans for the future."

The tears Suzannah had been holding in started to flow as she turned and looked at Zach. His gift was amazing. It meant so much to her, and Abby, and Edith, not to mention the entire town. "I can't believe you did this," she said.

"I've wanted to do something for a long time, and this just seems right. Keith was my best friend, and it's important to me that he's remembered. I figure since Edith is doing her part to keep his memory alive, now was a good time for me to do my part," he said.

Overcome with love, Suzannah hugged him close, which was a little difficult to do in their padded costumes. Still, she managed it. "You are such a wonderful man, and I love you very much."

"You are such a wonderful woman, and I love you very much," he teased back, then added softly. "Let's just hope you still love me once I'm no longer soft and squishy and don't have a full white beard. For all I know, you only love me because you think I'm Santa Claus."

She pretended to consider what he said. "I do love Santa Claus, but I also love the man he truly is. I will always love you," she assured him, leaning forward and kissing him.

The crowd cheered as Santa kissed Mrs. Claus back. He dipped her a little at the end of the kiss, causing an even bigger round of applause.

After a moment, Suzannah realized they had one special witness. She broke off the kiss and saw her daughter was standing next to them.

"So, Mom, it looks like my Christmas wish will come true," Abby said, beaming.

"It looks that way," Suzannah said. "Definitely looks that way."

Abby turned and hollered at her friend Stephie. "Hey, Stephie. My Christmas wish came true! I bet next year's Christmas wish will come true as well."

Puzzled, Suzannah looked at Zach, who shrugged and said, "I have no idea. She only told me about this year's wish."

Although she was a little afraid to ask, curiosity

finally got the best of her. "What is your Christmas wish for next year?"

The smirk on Abby's face was pure mischief. "I'm going to ask for a baby sister or brother!"

Suzannah laughed and admitted, "Well, you never know. This is Kringle. It's a magical place, so that Christmas wish might come true as well."

~

Dear Reader,

Readers are an author's life blood and the stories couldn't happen without you. Thank you so much for reading! If you enjoyed *A Perfect Christmas Wish,* I would so appreciate a review. You have no idea how much it means! Thank you, thank you.

Please turn the page for an excerpt of the next book in the series, *A Perfect Christmas Surprise* featuring Caleb and Ava's romance.

If you'd like to keep up with my latest releases, you can sign up for my newsletter @ https://loriwilde.com/subscribe/

To check out my other books, you can visit me on the web @ www.loriwilde.com.

Much love and light!

—Lori

EXCERPT: A PERFECT CHRISTMAS SURPRISE

Caleb Sutton walked into the lobby of the Kringle Animal Clinic, looked around, and bit back a curse.

Dogs were barking, cats meowing, and Christmas carols played loudly. The place was a madhouse, packed wall to wall with animals, all controlled to varying degrees by their owners.

Man, he hated surprises, and this was a big one.

"Hey, there, Caleb, welcome to the party." Zach Delaney was a fellow rancher, and currently dressed as Santa. The man who obviously a good sport to put up with this mess.

"Ho, ho, ho to you too." Caleb lifted his cowboy hat to scratch his head and grinned. "What's going on?"

"Pictures with Santa. Could you scooch over. You're in the shot," said a decidedly sexy female voice.

Caleb turned and looked at the speaker, did a double take and once again struggled to not curse. Man, this day was going downhill faster than an inner tube at Kringle Village's snow sled lanes. How in the world had he not seen *her* sooner?

Blond bombshell, Ava Miller stood behind a tripod holding a camera in one hand, the other hand cocked on her hip. She was dressed in some kind of crazy looking candy cane costume. And at the moment, she seemed more than a little annoyed at him.

"Please move," she repeated, waving to indicate he needed to step farther into the waiting area.

He tried to ignore the overwrought pounding of his stupid heart and took a few steps forward until he was certain he was no longer blocking her vantage point. "Is this okay?"

She chuffed under her breath, scowled and motioned him to keep on going.

He bit down on his tongue to keep from saying

anything negative and shuffled over another few inches. He didn't want to cause a scene and bother other people. Just because he would rather dance barefoot across hot stones than talk to Ava Miller didn't mean he had to right to ruin everyone else's day.

"Great. Thanks."

The cacophony, and Ava's presence, irritated the fire out of him, but right now, he needed to calm down. He had a million questions but didn't want to cause a dust up. Finally, he noticed a small chair tucked in the far corner and took a seat.

Trudy Manfred was sitting next to him with two small brown dogs, both dressed as little reindeers complete with antlers, wriggling in her arms.

In Caleb's opinion, the dogs looked a bit silly, but no way would he tell Trudy that.

"Hi, Caleb." Trudy beamed and shoved one of the dogs in his arms. "Mind holding Buttons?"

The questions appeared to be rhetorical, since Buttons was already licking his face, but manners required him to say, "Sure."

"It's nice Ava is back," Trudy said, patting the dog she still held. "Don't you think?"

Nice was the last word Caleb would have chosen. Still, he said, "Yes," because he'd been raised too well to voice his real feelings.

The truthfully, he was far from happy. He'd been happier when Ava stayed away from Kringle. It might be her hometown and her parents might still live here, but Ava Miller had caused him more problems than a coyote in a hen house. Throughout high school, they'd either been madly in love or madly in hate with each other. There had never been any middle ground.

She'd been his first girlfriend, his first love, and his first heartbreak. Yep, he'd had enough of Ava Miller to last him a lifetime.

A small yip brought his attention to the dog in his arms. Looked like Buttons was no happier about this situation than Caleb. He couldn't blame the fella. The dog did look ridiculous dressed like a reindeer.

"Good boy," he said, and scratched Buttons behind his ear. He glanced over at Zach, who looked about as happy as a rancher could when he was dressed as Santa. Caleb would bet his best horse that some woman had convinced poor Zach to pretend to be Santa. Just like some woman had dressed Buttons like a reindeer.

Just like Ava's mother, Marjorie, had convinced him to come to town to pick up some of the animals that had been dropped off at the vet. Marjorie and her husband Ted ran a dog rescue organization on a small piece of land on his ranch.

He'd donated the land to them years ago when it looked like he and Ava were getting married. After Ava left town, he'd just let them keep the land. No sense making a bad situation worse by being petty.

And odd pang of sadness pinged inside his chest and Caleb clenched his jaw.

The Millers' shelter, Kringle Kritter Rescue, was a great organization that helped local strays find loving homes. He'd agreed this morning to swing by the vet's office to pick up a few animals Marjorie had left here.

He hadn't known he'd be walking into a photo shoot with Ava behind the camera, or he would not have come.

"We are too agreeable, you and me," he muttered to Buttons. "Just look at us."

"The dog peered up at him with somber eyes.

"Who is to agreeable?" Trudy asked.

Thankfully, he was spared from answering because it was Trudy's turn. He helped her get her dogs settled on poor Zach's lap so they were ready for their picture, and then he returned to his seat. He deliberately avoided looking at Ava. He didn't need to look at her. He knew what she looked like. Even after several years, he still remembered every detail about her.

Her scent, her smile, the taste of those sweet cherry lips.

She was beautiful. Always had been. She had a smile that lit up a room and amazing brown eyes that seemed to sparkle when she found something funny, which was often. Ava liked to laugh, and she had great one.

He missed the laugh most of all.

"Caleb, can you help Trudy to her car?" This came from the vet, Chloe Anderson, who owned and operated the Kringle Animal Clinic. Caleb was a big fan of Chloe's. She was a smart lady and a terrific vet.

"Sure," he said, taking Buttons again when Trudy once more shoved the poor dog his way. He and Buttons were becoming good pals. He looked down at the little dog who seemed almost to roll his eyes. Caleb chuckled.

"What's funny?"

The question came from Ava, and Caleb shook his head. He wasn't getting drawn into that mess.

"Nothing worth mentioning," he said.

He kept his focus on Trudy and her dogs, helping the senior citizen outside and getting her settled in her car. After they were set, he started to walk back inside, but Trudy waved him back over to the car. She leaned through the open driver's side window and fixed him with a serious stare.

"You watch out, Caleb," Trudy said. "Lord knows, we all love Ava, but she'd bad for you. Take care of yourself."

With that, she gave him a quick pat on the cheek and then closed her window. Caleb watched her back out of the parking spot. Yeah, Trudy was right. No doubt about it.

Ava Miller was bad for him.

ABOUT THE AUTHOR

Lori Wilde is the New York Times, USA Today and Publishers' Weekly bestselling author of 90 works of romantic fiction. She's a three time Romance Writers' of America RITA finalist and has four times been nominated for Romantic Times Readers' Choice Award. She has won numerous other awards as well.

Her books have been translated into 26 languages, with more than four million copies of her books sold worldwide.

Her breakout novel, *The First Love Cookie Club*, has been optioned for a TV movie.

Lori is a registered nurse with a BSN from Texas Christian University. She holds a certificate in forensics, and is also a certified yoga instructor.

A fifth generation Texan, Lori lives with her husband, Bill, in the Cutting Horse Capital of the World; where they run Epiphany Orchards, a writing/creativity retreat for the care and enrichment of the artistic soul.

ALSO BY LORI WILDE

TEXAS RASCALS SERIES

Keegan

Matt

Nick

Kurt

Tucker

Kael

Truman

Dan

Rex

Clay

Jonah

Kringle, Texas Series

A Perfect Christmas Gift

A Perfect Christmas Wish

A Perfect Christmas Surprise

❀ Created with Vellum

Made in the USA
Columbia, SC
15 December 2019